I looked down and saw that Bradley's shoe was untied. I wondered how Andi could like someone who couldn't keep his shoes tied and who brought her flowers with the plastic still wrapped around them. Then it occurred to me that she'd like flowers that Bradley brought her even if they were wrapped in old newspapers. And that thought made me laugh. Which then made me cry.

Now That Andi's Gone

Karle Dickerson

To girls who've ever lost
someone they loved

Published by Willowisp Press
801 94th Avenue North, St. Petersburg, Florida 33702

Printed in the United States of America

2 4 6 8 10 9 7 5 3

ISBN 0-87406-676-X

One

"HOW do you know he likes you?" I demanded. "I haven't seen any signs."

My best friend, Andi Moreland, collapsed on my bed with the goofiest expression I'd ever seen. Her dark, curly hair flopped across her face, and she blew it off. "I just know," she said simply. She hugged herself and kicked her legs up a few times, as if she were riding an upside-down bicycle. "It's the way he looks at me."

"Oh, puleeze!" The whole thing was ridiculous. Sophomore boys don't like freshman girls, even if they are popular and cute like Andi. It was pretty simple. Andi was off in Andi-Land if she thought that Bradley Price really noticed her.

"No, really. I read about it in a magazine. The article was called 'How To Tell If He Likes You.' All the signs are there. He looks at me in history class. He says 'hi'—just like that—when I say 'hi' to him. He always seems to be at his locker at the same time we're at ours."

"So are three-quarters of the students at Riverview High School," I pointed out. "It's called 'passing period.'" I wasn't trying to ruin her fantasy. I was just being me. Practical Kimberly Lee Bowen.

"Really, Kimmie, you have no romance in your soul," said Andi. "None. Zero. Zip. If you did, you'd see that Bradley likes me."

I frowned and tapped my pencil on my desk. I had to get her off the subject. We were wasting homework time. "Fine. So Bradley Price, world's cutest guy, is certifiably insane about you. He can't live without you." I summed up what we had accomplished in the last half-hour of our math session. "But now, what are we going to do about your algebra grade?"

Andi sighed and crawled off my bed, looking much the way my basset hound, Basil, looks when I drag him outside in the rain. She would do anything to avoid homework. As for me, I kind of like doing homework. Of course, Andi and I are total opposites, which my mom says is probably why we're best friends.

"Okay, okay," said Andi. "I'll stop talking about Bradley. Actually, I'd like to beam Ms. Sharp off the face of the earth instead, but I'll do her stupid homework problems."

"And bring up your algebra grade so you won't get kicked off the freshman cheerleading squad," I reminded her.

Andi jumped up, throwing out her arms. "Who's the team that can't be beat? Who's the—"

She stopped mid-cheer when she saw my face. "Whoops. I'm sitting down now. I've picked up my pencil. I'm looking at my homework."

I watched her briefly to make sure she would stick to her algebra for at least a few minutes without bringing up Bradley. But stick to it she did, and after a bit I turned to my own homework. I was taking an honors English class and we had to answer questions in essay form on a book we'd just finished reading. It struck me that getting Andi to do her homework was a lot harder.

I had just started my topic sentence when Andi said, "I wonder if I should get Mwoop a friend."

She was talking about Mwoop, her pet guinea pig. Most of the kids our age had hamsters and guinea pigs when we were in elementary school. But then we outgrew them. Not Andi. Her house was filled with pets with totally weird names. She had mice and hamsters, two dogs, and some ducks. Mwoop was the latest addition. She gave him that name because "mwoop" was the squeak he made. Now Andi was interrupting to tell me she wanted another guinea pig.

"You're actually going to take on another pet?" I asked, shaking my head. "Your parents will totally flip out."

"I like my animals. They're my best friends," Andi said defensively.

I set down my pencil. "Thanks a lot. I thought I was your best friend."

In an instant, Andi was up. She threw her arms around me. "I didn't mean it that way. You *are* my best friend. You've always been. You'll always be."

I almost fell off my chair in shock. Andi is the nicest girl and greatest best friend in the world. She has more friends than anyone I know, and she always goes out of her way to make sure I know I'm her best. But she hardly ever gets serious. She never says things like that—even though we've been best friends since we were together in daycare! But I didn't get a chance to say anything back because my door suddenly crashed open and my three-year-old twin brothers, Matthew and Jared, whirled in.

"Andi, Andi, Andi," they chanted. "Play with us!"

That did it. Andi dropped her pencil and scooped up my brothers, one in each arm.

"Not now—" I started.

"Oh, come on, Kimmie," Andi protested. "Just for a while. These guys need a little wrestling." She disappeared out my door.

I shook my head and looked at the ceiling for a sec. But I had to smile. Being friends with Andi meant you never knew what was coming next.

* * * * *

The next morning I got up early and looked outside to see if I could tell what kind of day it would be. No surprise. After all, it was January, and January in Iowa means gray and cold.

I showered, pulled on tights under my jeans, and tugged a black sweater over my head. I dried my long, dark hair that never curled right and spritzed on some Crazy About You cologne. Andi had given it to me for my birthday last month, but I'd never used it. For a finishing touch, I put on the crystal snowflake pendant that my dad gave me a long time ago.

When I got downstairs, I could see that Mom was frazzled. She was trying to feed the twins breakfast, all the while trying not to get any of it on her stylish navy suit. "Oh, Kimmie, give me a hand, will you?" She was trying to convince Jared that hot cereal was exactly what he wanted. He didn't look persuaded, and neither did Matthew.

I slid into a chair by Matthew. "Eat," I said, wrapping my hand around his. I tried to guide the spoon toward his mouth.

"I can do it myself," Matthew complained. He knocked the spoon away.

"Then show me," I countered. For once, Matthew cooperated and fed himself the whole spoonful.

"Where's Dad?" I asked, turning toward my mom.

"He left for the airport early to catch a flight to Chicago. Big meeting," Mom said in a crisp voice that told me she was mentally already at her office.

My dad's the vice president of this company that makes all kinds of gifts, the kind you see in gift and greeting card stores. He travels a lot, and it's kind of hard on my mom and me. Getting two three-year-olds ready for daycare can be wild. Like this morning. It took forever to get them to eat. Jared knocked over his bowl and cereal splattered everywhere. Mom had to change her suit. She said that that there was no way she'd show up at her real estate office wearing a glob of dried cereal stuck to her jacket.

Finally, my mom and I got the twins fed and bundled into heavy jackets. I helped Mom buckle them into their car seats and gave each twin a kiss. Jared likes kisses. Matthew doesn't. I waved goodbye as the car pulled away, zipped up my ski parka, and walked toward Andi's house.

She lives only one street over, but her house is at the opposite end of mine. Rubbing my hands together for warmth, I walked faster.

Andi's house is neat. It's white with green shutters and lots of flowers. My mom says she doesn't know how Andi's mother manages to keep her flowers blooming long after everyone else's die for the winter. Today I admired some yellow flowers blooming inside the windows. It seemed right that flowers would stay in bloom longer at Andi's house. I don't ever think I knew any family that laughs as much as hers.

Even though I was a little late, Andi wasn't waiting for me at her door. I rang the doorbell. Geez. I hoped the Morelands weren't oversleeping. But when I pressed my ear to the door, I could hear signs of life. Andi's laugh. Then her big brother Alex's laugh. Then her dad's booming laugh. Mr. Moreland threw open the door.

"Kimmie Bowen!" he said, his whole face caught up in a huge smile. "How nice to see you this morning," he added, like it was a big surprise. Like he hadn't seen me practically every school morning since Andi had been born.

"I'm coming, I'm coming. I'm late. I know it," shouted Andi. She was wearing her blue-and-white cheerleading sweater over a white turtleneck. Her curly hair spilled over her headband. After jamming herself into a bulky jacket, she brushed past her dad, kissed him, then shoved a bagel in her mouth. "Hi, Kimmie," she said, the words muffled by the bagel. Her earrings jingled in the cool wind swirling around us.

"Algebra book?" I asked.

Andi darted back inside, then reappeared

with the book. She shoved it into her shapeless book bag. The bagel still stuck out of her mouth.

"What would we do without you!" her dad exclaimed. "She never listens to us." He shook his head, winked at me, and shut the door. Andi and I were off to school.

"I got home last night, and one of my ducks had caught his foot under the wire," Andi said. "Anyway, I had to doctor him up, and I was so worried about him, I forgot that I had an essay due in history today." She groaned.

"Andi," I said with a sigh, "you're about to become an ex-cheerleader."

Andi did this little half-skip and pirouette, her book bag straps flapping. "I'll figure something out. I always do."

I couldn't argue the point. Andi always managed to worm her way out of every scrape she landed in. Last year was a perfect example. Ignoring school rules about unauthorized pets, she sneaked Desert Dog—one of her ducks—to school. But Desert Dog wriggled out of his box and waddled down the hall. Kids were going crazy and Andi was flipping out, sure that someone would step on the duck before she could catch him. I was flipping out, too, sure that Andi would be suspended.

Of course, that's not what happened. Somehow, she ended up surrounded by a big group of kids and a stern-faced science teacher. But before anyone could say anything, Andi launched into this off-the-cuff lesson about ducks and their care. It sounds dull, but Andi made it interesting. Everyone was fascinated. And no one gave a thought to the rule she broke.

I was about to tell her that she might not always be that lucky when she said, "Melissa Hendricks called me last night. She said that some of the girls are going to meet after school and help plan the freshman dance. She asked me to come. You could come too."

"No, thanks," I said, trying not to get annoyed.

Melissa Hendricks was on the cheerleading squad with Andi. She was your basic competitive, out-for-herself type. I wondered how Andi could stand her, but then, Andi liked everyone and everyone liked her.

"Are you sure?" Andi asked. "I mean, if we're going to go and watch everyone dance anyway, we might as well have good decorations to look at and good munchies to eat."

I snorted. "Who said I was going?

Besides, even if I do, *you'll* be dancing and *I'll* be watching—and in charge of taking numbers for your next dance partners."

Andi laughed her famous laugh. "You're so funny. You danced a lot at our eighth-grade dance last year. Anyway, I wouldn't want to go to the dance without you. Please be on the committee?"

"Oh, all right." I never could turn down an Andi request.

"Hey—there's Shannon and Charley."

"Hey, Andi . . . Kimmie," Shannon Olson called. She and Charlene Hamlin lived in our neighborhood. They were both pretty nice girls. We had all played together when we were in elementary school. Now they were into drama, and Andi hated drama, so we didn't hang around together that much anymore.

Rehearsals for the spring play were just starting, and Andi asked Charley and Shannon how they were going. They started talking a mile a minute. Every few sentences would be punctuated by Andi's laugh. Then Charley mentioned Bradley Price's name.

"He asked about you at drama rehearsal yesterday afternoon," Charley said. "Wanted to know exactly where you live."

Andi put her hands up to her throat and squealed delightedly. "He did not! I'm dying! Cardiac arrest!" She whirled toward me. "See? What did I tell you, Kimmie?"

"You win," I said, my smile hiding the dread that was gnawing inside me. Now there was no denying it. Somehow Andi had beaten the odds—again. Maybe this boy she had a crush on really *did* have a crush on her.

"Maybe I should join drama," Andi said.

I could tell the wheels in her brain were turning swiftly. I fell behind the group just a bit, not certain why I felt the way I did. It isn't that I don't like boys. They're okay. One day, I might even want a boyfriend myself. And it wasn't that Bradley isn't an okay person, even if he is too tall and thin for my taste.

It's just that I've invested a lot of time in my best friend and I see how girls around my school get all weird when they have boyfriends. If Bradley really started liking Andi, she would be so busy with him that I'd probably never see her. Our friendship would be a mess.

My mind was racing as we turned up Riverview High's front walk. I sighed. The thing is, friendship takes work. And since it seemed obvious that Andi couldn't think clearly about all this stuff, the work would be up to me.

I didn't exactly have a plan, but I guessed I would start by making sure that Andi waited a while before she started weirding out over a boyfriend. Which meant I'd have to figure out a way to keep Bradley Price from getting in the way of our best friendship.

If things were reversed, Andi would do the same. She would do whatever it took to guard our friendship, wouldn't she?

Two

OVER the next few days, I tried to devise all kinds of ways to get rid of Bradley for Andi. I kept picturing the way she got all turbo-charged when she talked about him. But, unfortunately, while my mind was good at processing stuff like algebra, it wasn't much good at figuring out ways to dispose of people.

A week later, I decided that maybe I'd get lucky, and the company where Bradley's mom or dad worked would move his family somewhere far away. I was picturing a tearful goodbye scene when my Western Civilizations teacher, Mr. Blake, interrupted my thoughts. He reminded me that my attention should be in the classroom, not out the window. I blushed and tried to focus on his lecture. Of course, by the time I met up with Andi just before homeroom,

I was no further along in my Dump Bradley scheme.

"Ugh. Algebra was the worst," she said, dumping a pile of books into the locker we shared.

"How was your quiz?" I asked.

Andi shrugged. "Dunno." She tilted her head and looked at me. "You know something, though? I've decided I want to go to college."

I shoved my own books into the locker without missing a beat. Some people might not be able to handle the way Andi switched subjects so quickly. But I was used to it.

"Last week you weren't going to college ever," I reminded her. "You were going to join a crew and go on a sailing adventure around the world." I didn't point out that the week before that she was going to become a professional horseshoer.

Andi giggled. "Oh, puleeze. I get seasick." A toss of her head indicated she had definitely nixed that plan.

"Okay, so why the change of heart?" I asked. I wrestled a science book out of the locker.

"I want to go to learn how to be a TV anchor on a news show," Andi announced.

"That means college."

"How did you decide that?" I asked. I tried to picture Andi in a royal blue suit with huge earrings, smiling from behind one of those newsroom desks on TV. Nope. I couldn't see it.

Andi shrugged. "I was just thinking about how Ms. Sharp was so boring. How I wished I was anywhere but in algebra. Like at the dance. Dancing with—"

I cringed and slammed our locker door shut.

"Then I had to turn in my quiz—"

"You were thinking all this while you were supposed to be taking your quiz?" I asked. There was no doubt about it—my best friend was doomed, both for her grades and for cheerleading.

Andi nodded and adjusted her books. "That's when I decided that I'd probably gotten a *D* on my quiz. And that you're right—maybe it's time I started being more serious. Serious like news anchors are when they're reporting something really horrible."

Actually, maybe her idea was good—even perfect. If Andi got serious about a high-powered career she might put Bradley out of her mind forever.

But just then, guess who walked by? And Andi looked anything but how a girl should look who's put a guy out of her mind forever. I threw a mega-glare at Bradley, but he didn't notice. He was too busy looking at her. Oh, puleeze! I looked at him, trying to figure out what Andi saw in him.

He was way tall. He had boring brown hair, ho-hum eyes. His sweater was stretched out and baggy. If you asked me, he looked like a rumpled brown grocery bag. Not the stuff of romance.

Andi giggled as we passed him on our way to homeroom. Puleeze! My heart sunk right to my sneakers again. Getting Andi to forget about Bradley was going to be harder then I thought.

The rest of the morning, I tried to work on Dump Bradley schemes. At lunch, just when Andi and I were about to plan our weekend, Bradley came up and started talking with her. It didn't take long until I felt weird, like I was spying on their conversation or something. So I pretended I wanted another carton of milk at the snack shack. There I was, drinking a carton of milk I didn't want, while Andi gazed into Bradley's eyes.

Give me a break! I was ready to throw

up. I was never more glad to hear the lunch bell ring. Bradley waved goodbye and walked off.

"He was telling me about his part in the spring play," Andi told me as we walked to our locker. "I never realized that so much work went into the whole thing. There's so much you have to think about all the time."

"I try never to think about it," I said, shaking my head and spinning the locker combination. For one thing, I didn't like drama. Drama meant being on a stage in front of people. For another, anything connected with Bradley didn't interest me.

I threw open the door—and came eyeball to eyeball with the grossest white rat I'd ever seen. It was in a little cage, and its pink eyes never left mine. I resisted the urge to scream or even jump back. I knew who was to blame.

"Andi, if this is another of your horrible jokes—"

But I got no further because Andi was totally cracking up. At me. I glared at her.

"Sorry," she said, trying to stifle her giggles. "But you should have seen your face."

"Not funny. On a scale of one to ten, this ranks a two." I made a *bzzzt!* noise like the kind you hear on a game show when the answer's wrong.

"It wasn't a joke," Andi protested. "That rat was imprisoned in our science lab. It was a lab animal. I freed it."

I looked pointedly at the cage. "He looks anything but free to me. He's trapped in a little cage that's crammed inside a dark locker."

Andi stuck the tip of a finger into the cage and made little kissy noises. "But he'll *be* free. I'm taking him home to live with me. His name's Griswold. Mrs. Harris was going to feed Griswold to a snake. I saved him."

"Does Mrs. Harris know this?"

"Well, no . . ." Andi admitted. "I'm hoping she won't notice. You know . . . out of sight, out of mind."

"Bad move, Andi," I said, shaking my head. "You could get in a lot of trouble."

"Well, maybe. But even if I could sneak him back into the classroom, he would only become snake bait again. He'd be dead in a flash." Suddenly, she thumped her head with the heel of her hand. "Oh, man. I just had another thought. Now the snake will be hungry. I'll have to think of something else to feed it."

"Don't panic," I muttered. "I'll help you think of something."

I was scowling, but actually, I was starting to feel okay again. This was what I was used to: Andi in trouble, and me trying to use my brains to figure a way out for her. But just then Melissa Hendricks turned up. Another rat.

"Hey, Andi, you coming to the freshman dance meeting after school?"

Andi looked at me. "I guess so, if Kimmie is coming."

I nodded. "I'll be there," I mumbled. It was hard to say no when Andi looked at me like that.

Melissa looked like she couldn't care less about me, but I could tell she was glad that Andi was coming. I was used to that, being invisible next to Andi. I turned my back to Melissa and dug around in the locker, pretending that I was in a hurry.

"Hey, there's a rat in there," Melissa said, peering into the locker and shivering. "Isn't that the rat that was in the science lab this morning?"

Andi nodded and closed the locker door. "Don't tell anyone."

"They have the grossest tails," Melissa added. She looked at me, then back at Andi. "See you after school," she said as she started down the crowded hall.

Andi gave me a look. "You don't think she'll accidentally blurt it out, do you?" she asked helplessly. "I'd better go talk to her."

As I watched her go, I wished for the zillionth time that Andi didn't attract attention so easily. I wouldn't have to worry about Melissa Hendricks conning Andi into things like dance committees—or about Bradley Price trying to swipe my best friend out from under my nose.

You are being totally immature, Kimberly Bowen, I told myself sternly as I hurried toward science class. Andi can certainly have other friends. She always has—and so have you. And Bradley's not the first guy she's had a crush on. But what made this weird, I thought, is that this time, the guy seems to like her back.

While Mr. Lieber lectured us about prehistoric creatures like trilobites, I concentrated on my plans. I realized that I'd probably never get Bradley to back off on Andi. I'd have to work on Andi instead. I'd talk with her later. Today. After dance committee. At my house.

By the time school was over, I felt cheerful again. I headed to the classroom where the dance committee met. Melissa was in charge and couldn't get anything started.

Andi didn't seem to be paying attention and in the end, we hadn't decided a thing. The best part was leaving.

The next step was the rat. Andi and I sneaked it out of our locker and put it in her book bag. Then while I kept an eye out for trouble, Andi whisked the empty cage back to her science classroom. The idea was to make Mrs. Harris think it had escaped. I expected to get caught any minute, but nothing happened. Typically, Andi's luck was holding.

Finally, we set off for the walk home. I tried to ignore the faint scratching noise coming from Andi's book bag. I can't say I was happy about what we were doing, but I was happy that Andi was happy.

"Hooray. It's Thursday. That means tomorrow's Friday. Then comes the week-end," Andi said as we left the school grounds.

"Brilliant, Professor Moreland," I said. "But you're right. And we need a weekend. It's been a long week."

"By the way, we need to stop by Pet City on the way home from school," Andi in-formed me. "Mwoop's all out of guinea pig pellets."

"Geez. Mwoop sure eats a lot," I complained. I just wanted to get home. It was already late, and the sky was getting gloomy. Andi always got carried away talking to Mrs. L, the lady who worked at Pet City. Sometimes we stayed there for what seemed like hours.

I sighed and adjusted my book bag. Pet City was in a small mall along with Video Bandits and Planet Pizza, only a block from Riverview High. First thing I did when we entered was to clap my hands over my ears. The squeaking! The squawking! The puppies barked, and Vincent, a big Amazon parrot, yelled, "Take a chill pill!!" Mrs. L's daughter had taught him that.

I thought about trying to persuade Andi to leave the rat here. But I knew she'd never go for it and I wasn't in the mood to fight her.

"Hey, Mrs. L!" Andi called, peeling off her ski jacket and pushing up the sleeves of her cheerleading sweater.

Mrs. L was standing on a stool, getting a beanbag dog bed down from a high shelf. Her eyes twinkled and her face broke into a wide grin when she saw Andi.

"What's up?" she asked, climbing down from the stool. "Did you try those vitamin drops I recommended?"

Andi stopped to peer in at Vincent, who preened his colorful feathers when she stuck her finger in the cage. Vincent would bite anyone else who did that.

"Yeah," Andi said. "You were right. Mwoop's coat looks shinier. Now I need some more food for him."

Mrs. L nodded and went to get a big bag of guinea pig food. Andi bought a bag from Mrs. L. about every two weeks or so. The two of them started talking pig, so I wandered over to look at the kittens. Too bad I was allergic. I hoped I didn't start sneezing.

Finally, some other customers came in and Andi said goodbye. As we walked down the street, she talked about Mwoop and the guinea pig family she wanted to start. She said she was going to read up on rats, too, just in case it turned out there was a possibility the thing in her book bag would get along with her other rodent.

Normally, we stopped at my house after school. But I insisted that Andi drop the rat off at her place first. To make sure she hurried, I didn't even go inside. And when she came out, I didn't ask her anything about it. My mind was on what I was going to say about Bradley.

When we finally got to my house, I didn't

even think about offering Andi a snack. I hurried her upstairs and down the hall toward my room. It was just my bad luck that we had to pass Dad's camcorder case propped against the wall.

"What's that? A video camera?" Andi asked.

I glanced at it. "Yeah," I said impatiently.

Andi's eyes grew wide. "I didn't know you had one of these."

"I don't. It's my dad's."

"Cool. Do you know how it works?"

"Sort of," I answered slowly. My dad had shown me so I could tape him and my mom dancing to "their" song one night. But I also knew my dad would kill me if I touched it without asking. It had just come back from the repair shop after one of the twins had used it to prop up some race car tracks. Someone had stepped on it; no one would admit to it.

"Can we try it out?" Andi asked.

"I really shouldn't even touch it," I said.

"Just for a minute?"

One look at Andi, and I knew she wouldn't be put off. Maybe if I showed her how it worked, she'd slow down long enough to listen to me.

"Okay," I said reluctantly, picking up the

camera and taking it in my room. I could always erase anything we taped. My parents would never even have to know I'd used it.

Andi tossed her parka on a chair and flipped on my stereo, while I carefully set the video camera on my dresser. I studied the buttons and dials and whatnot. The whole time, Andi chattered nonstop about my bulletin board. It was covered with pictures of the two of us. Ticket stubs from the riding stables where Andi had talked me into renting a fast horse for an hour. Programs, a birthday card. Our T-ball team photo from when we were in second grade.

Aha! I thought. It looked like Andi had forgotten about the video camera. Now maybe I could bring up Bradley and talk to her about him. But just as I opened my mouth to say something, a song blasted out of the stereo. Andi leaped onto the bed, lights dancing in her eyes.

"My favorite song! 'Let's Go Wild!' Have you seen the new music video of this one? It's Rae Ann's best! She's such a hot dancer!"

Andi started moving like Rae Ann did. It was all very well for a rock star like Rae Ann to do, but it was another thing altogether to see Andi do it. For one thing, Andi had more energy than Rae Ann, and more cheerleader-like moves. And she had way more hair.

"Come on, Kimmie! Turn on the camera. Let's dance to this one!" Andi pleaded.

She didn't need me. She was dancing enough for both of us, her head swirling wildly, her whole body moving to the frenzied tempo.

I sighed, aimed the camera at the bed, flipped on the switch, and hopped up next to Andi. Maybe she'd tire herself out, and then we could get down to the serious business of talking about Bradley.

We jumped, we twisted, we turned. Andi pretended she was holding a microphone, and she kept shoving it in my face. "Can't hear you," she yelled.

I sang as we jumped, totally wrecking my striped, tailored covers. I was getting exhausted, but still Andi kept dancing, and still we kept belting out the words with Rae Ann to "Let's Go Wild!"

When the song finally ended, I collapsed. Andi brushed her hair from her eyes and started laughing in between catching her breath.

"You look fried!" she said, peeling off her

cheerleader sweater. She wore a blouse underneath, and it didn't even look wrinkled.

"Very funny," I said, stumbling over to turn off the camera. "I'll bet Rae Ann didn't look much better when she was finished."

"Just think, Kimmie! We did it!" said Andi. "We made our very first dance video." Her eyes lit up. "Hey! That's it," she said, snapping her fingers. "Here's what we can do for our careers. Forget college. We'll be rock singers. You and me. You won't have to study so hard. All we have to do is think of a name for ourselves."

"What about wanting to be a TV anchor?" I asked.

Andi shook her head. "Too serious."

"Enough!" I yelled. "I've had enough. I don't want to be a rock singer!" Andi looked crushed, so I softened. "*You* be a rock singer. I'll be your . . . your manager or something. I'd collapse if I had to dance like that all the time. Besides, I'd never be able to get up in front of people," I said, desperately trying to steer the conversation back where I wanted it.

"You'd do fine," Andi protested. "Come on. Let's go watch our video. You'll see."

Just then the phone rang. Andi's mom. She called at five every day to let Andi know it was time to come home to help with dinner.

Andi grabbed the phone and talked briefly. She hung up and sighed. "Darn. I've got to go." She squiggled into her parka. "I really wanted to watch our video right now, but I guess it'll have to wait."

I was secretly grateful, because I couldn't imagine not getting caught when we stuck the video into the VCR downstairs. But all I said was that it was no big deal. We could watch it anytime.

As Andi galloped down the stairs, I shook my head. I'd wasted precious time making a stupid video when what I really wanted was to talk to her. Now it would have to wait—again.

Best friends were a ton of work, I thought to myself as I drifted off to sleep that night. Especially one as hyper as Andi.

Three

THE next morning, Mom reminded me to return Andi's cheerleading sweater on my way to school. "Oh, yes, and don't forget that we'll be going to Grandpa Pete's tonight after we pick up Dad from the airport."

My shoulders slumped. With all my concern about Andi and Bradley, I'd forgotten that Grandpa Pete was leaving for a three-week cruise, and that we were going to his place for a send-off dinner.

Mom seemed tense and preoccupied as she wrestled with getting breakfast down Jared and Matthew, so I didn't ask if I could skip the dinner. I like Grandpa Pete, but I just didn't want to go to his condo tonight. I mean, I'd planned to try to talk with Andi tonight. Oh well, I guessed another day wouldn't really matter.

After Mom and the twins headed off to the daycare center, I turned down the heat and shut off the lights. Then I started my walk to Andi's. The sky was gray and the wind cold, so I walked quickly, shivering in spite of my thick jacket. The lights were all on at Andi's, and I hurried toward them, drawn like a moth.

Mrs. Moreland opened the door before I even rang the doorbell. "Kimmie!" she exclaimed, her whole face turning up in a big smile. "Come on in."

"Hi," I said, stepping inside. A blast of warmth hit me in the face. It felt terrific. The house smelled like hot cocoa, and in the background, I could hear barks and other sounds of Andi's animals. "Is Andi ready?"

"She's feeding those animals of hers. Have a cup of hot cocoa," Mrs. Moreland said, turning toward the kitchen.

I doubted there was time, but I nodded and stepped into the Morelands' kitchen. This was maybe my favorite place in the whole world. Mr. Moreland had remodeled the kitchen, and it looked like an old farmhouse kitchen—the kind I saw on the covers of the home magazines in the grocery store. The far wall was covered with worn brick, and there was an old-fashioned hearth with a fire blazing in it. Mrs. Moreland had hung lots of copper pots from the beams overhead. There was a big picture window behind the sink, and of course there were flowers and plants everywhere.

"Hey, you," said Andi's brother Alex from the breakfast table. "How's it going?"

I've always liked Alex. He's a junior at the high school. Whenever I see him there, he says hi. I asked him about basketball (he's on our junior varsity team), and he said it was going okay. Then he got up to finish getting ready for school.

Mrs. Moreland fussed around me, pouring hot cocoa and asking me about school. I answered her questions, welcoming the attention. My mom always seems so busy in the mornings. So does my dad, for that matter. I guess it's because of the twins.

I held my hands in front of the fire, then glanced at the kitchen clock. What was taking Andi so long? We'd be late for school—not for the first time.

"Andi and her animals. It takes her almost a half-hour to take care of them in the mornings," Mrs. Moreland said, her eyes following mine to the clock.

I sat at the table and sipped the last of

my cocoa. Finally, Andi came charging into the kitchen, breathless. "Almost ready," she said, grabbing a cup of cocoa before she whirled out of the room again.

"Come on, we'll be late," I complained.

"I'm hurrying," Andi said, her voice fading as she retreated down the hall. She returned a minute later. "I can't find my cheerleading sweater."

Oops. Despite Mom's reminder, I'd forgotten to bring it. "It's at my house," I said guiltily.

"Oh, well." Andi wasn't fazed. She grabbed Alex's letterman jacket. I wondered if Alex would mind. Probably not. Alex never got mad about anything.

A few minutes later, we were on our way.

"Hooray, it's Friday!" Andi crowed as we neared the school. Right inside the gate, she dropped to one knee and yelled, "YES!"

I smiled to show that I was psyched about the weekend too, though I wasn't thrilled about going to Grandpa Pete's.

"Time to plan," Andie commanded. "What are we going to do this weekend?" Andi looked at me like she really expected me to come up with some fantastic new idea. I never did. It was always Andi who had the great ideas.

"Um, how about if we go to the library?" I said, my voice trailing off. It was a lame idea, and I knew it.

Andi's sigh confirmed it. "Boring with a capital *B*. We did that last week. I mean, what can we do that's *fun*?"

"Well, for starters, tonight's out," I said, explaining about my family's plans to see Grandpa Pete.

"It's out for me, too," said Andi. "My parents are taking me to a movie. But I'll come by tomorrow and maybe we can get someone to drive us to the ice-skating rink. We haven't skated in ages."

I nodded. Ice-skating. Of course. It was perfect. Now, why didn't I think of that! I was lucky to have Andi for a best friend, I thought for the zillionth time. She always thought of the perfect thing to do.

We reached our locker and I asked Andi what movie her family was going to see.

"Oh, probably something majorly dull."

Andi waited for me to spin the tumbler and get my books out. Then she threw a couple of her books in and closed the locker door with a thwack.

"You know my parents," she continued. "There will be all kinds of good movies playing in town, but they'll find something that's too weird for words. I wish you could come along and be bored with me."

I laughed. "So do I. We'll have to exchange boredom stories when we get together tomorrow."

Andi and I said goodbye and headed off in opposite directions. For me, the day was already dragging. I was sure it must be for Andi, too. But every time I ran into her at our locker she was as upbeat as ever. That was like a talent or something, I thought.

Finally, the bell rang at 3:15 and I wasted no time getting to our locker. I grinned when I saw Andi. She had beaten me there by a few seconds and was already unloading some books.

"Looks like it's about to rain or snow or something," I said gloomily, looking out the glass doors at the end of the hall.

Andi laughed. Even the gloomiest winter day in Iowa didn't get her down. Nothing. I was about to make a comment about it when I saw Bradley walking toward us. He had a slip of paper in his hand.

"I got a new locker assignment," he said, looking kind of embarrassed.

I narrowed my eyes at him, but Andi flashed him one of her goofiest smiles. "That's great."

"My . . . uh, other one was sticking all the time," he said, watching her intently. He started working the combination of a locker just two doors away from ours.

I wanted to throw up. It was easy to see that Bradley had finagled a new locker so he could be near Andi. Today, he looked more like a used grocery bag than ever! But Andi didn't seem to think so. The two of them kept looking at each other.

"I'll meet you by the door," I mumbled, and I took off.

I waited by the front door for a while, watching students zip their jackets as they prepared to step outside. It had just started to rain. I shivered and waited, fuming more and more with each passing minute. What could they possibly be talking about for so long? I wondered.

When Andi finally appeared, she was practically floating. Her face was lit up, and her smile was goofier than ever, if that was possible.

"Bradley asked me to the freshman dance," she whispered excitedly. Then she lightly jabbed me on the shoulder to punctuate what she'd just said.

I pasted on a false smile and said "Great!" But I was annoyed. If not for Andi,

I would never have agreed to be on the dance committee, much less go to the dance. And now she would be going with Bradley. I looked away. "We'd better get a move on. It's really starting to pour. I wish we had a ride home," I grumbled. "Alex isn't driving today, is he?" I asked hopefully.

Andi shook her head, and we stepped into the rain. "No such luck. His car isn't running, and anyway, he's staying after for basketball practice. So what? I like the rain."

"I don't," I muttered sourly.

We headed home without talking much. I kept my head down, so that the rain wouldn't get in my face. Andi tilted hers upward and caught drops on her tongue.

As we walked by Pet City, Andi waved cheerfully at Mrs. L, who was arranging a guinea pig display in the front window.

"I really think Mwoop needs a friend. He seems so lonely," Andi said, pausing to watch the guinea pigs nose around in the shavings.

"Your mother will kill you if you bring home any more animals," I said, watching the rain leave icy tracks on the pet store window.

"Yeah, maybe," Andi said cheerfully. But

she kept her eyes locked on the clump of furry pigs climbing around in the shavings. "See that little gray one? How do you think Mwoop would like her?"

I didn't say anything, and I was relieved that she didn't make a move to go into the store. Best friend or not, I could only take so many days cruising Pet City.

"Let's go," Andi said. She was quiet, and we didn't talk for almost two blocks. But as we approached my street, she sighed and said, "Something's bugging you, Kimmie."

"Not really," I said.

"Bradley," Andi stated flatly. "You're bugged about Bradley."

"No." I tried to make my voice sound unconcerned, but it came out a little bit higher than usual. "Why should I be?"

"You're bugged that I told him I'd go with him to the dance," she said. She looked me in the eye.

"You're just imagining that." I lied some more. "It wasn't like I was dying to go to the dance anyway."

"You don't have to hide it from me. I know you. You're totally ticked," Andi said softly. "You don't have to be, though. I told him I'd go with him, but that I wanted to hang out with you too. He said that was cool."

I felt weird. That was pretty nice of Bradley, I had to admit.

But still . . . he was taking away my best friend, no matter how you looked at it. I couldn't think of anything to say. Too many emotions were tumbling around inside me.

I shook my head. "Well, we're at my street," I mumbled. "Got to get ready to go to my grandpa's. I guess I'll see you tomorrow."

Andi lifted her chin. "You're not mad?"

I thought about it for a second. Was it anger I was feeling? Not exactly. It was just a weird feeling that our friendship had changed. Just a little, maybe. But I didn't like it.

I slowly let out my breath. "No, I'm not mad," I said truthfully. "I'll try to explain it to you tomorrow when you come over, okay?"

Andi reached over and squeezed my shoulder. "Okay. See you then."

I watched Andi as she walked off. Her hair swung from side to side. Suddenly, she whirled around and waved goodbye again. I waved, then turned and walked heavily toward my house. I wished I had figured out a way to go to the movies with Andi. Then maybe I could have talked with her, and things wouldn't have felt so weird.

* * * * *

As it turned out, going to Grandpa Pete's that night wasn't so bad. He's a great storyteller. My mom says he talks too much, but I like the way he jokes and gestures when he explains something. I got so caught up in his stories, I didn't have time to think about Andi and Bradley.

We wound up staying so late, I thought I'd fall sound asleep right on his living room floor. I did fall asleep in the car on the way home and couldn't remember stumbling up to my room and into bed.

But something woke me out of a deep sleep in the middle of the night. I lay still, listening to my heart pound for a few seconds. For some reason, I was frightened. Maybe I'd just had a nightmare that I couldn't remember. Maybe there was a burglar in the house. But no. If there were a burglar in the house, the dog would be up. Basil would be barking in a frenzy, but the house was absolutely still.

I reached for the water glass beside my bed and took a sip. I realized I was breathing weird—short little gasps. I hadn't wakened scared in the night like this since I was a little girl. I resisted the urge to run to my parents' room.

"Nightmare," I murmured to myself. "Stupid dream." Just the same, I got up and quietly called for Basil. He trotted into my room and leaped happily onto my bed. He smelled like wet dog—probably he'd gone out for a midnight romp in the rain through his doggie door—but his doggie body was comforting. Just for good measure, I turned on the radio. Rae Ann's voice crooned softly in the air around me. It seemed like forever before I could get to sleep again.

* * * * *

I opened my eyes early the next morning and came face to face with my pillow. I'd rolled onto it during the night, and now my face was smooshed into it. Tossing the pillow to the end of my bed, I got up.

Basil had slipped out at some point, and I heard him bark at something in the room next door. Probably the twins. Already they were quarreling with each other. They were always up at the crack of dawn. I slipped into their room, then led them downstairs, where I turned on Saturday morning cartoons and poured them some dry cereal. Maybe Mom and Dad could sleep in just a little and they wouldn't feel so hassled today. Then maybe they'd drive Andi and me to Skate World.

I went back to my room and decided to get my chores out of the way. Maybe my mom or dad had some work they wanted me to do so I could earn extra money for a new Rae Ann CD. In a while, I'd call Andi. We'd go ice-skating, and afterward, hang around the snack shop and drink hot cocoa, and then we'd talk. I'd try to explain to her about how I felt about her going out with Bradley.

With the day planned, I started to work on my room—no small task. My books were piled everywhere, Andi's sweater was still on the floor where she'd tossed it after doing our dance video. I'd have to remember to get it back to her.

As I made up my bed, a thought suddenly struck me—what if Andi hadn't wanted to do a dance video at all? What if she was just looking for a way to avoid talking to me about Bradley? The more I thought about it, the more sure I was that that was it, and the more sure I was, the madder I got. She'd known all along that he was going to ask her out, and she didn't want to talk about it with me! *She was freezing me out.* She'd never done that before. We'd always shared everything.

Just as I suspected: Bradley was already messing with my friendship with Andi.

"That's it!" I decided and picked up my phone. I punched in Andi's number. She had her own line and usually answered right away. It rang four times before her answering machine clicked on. Weird that she wasn't picking up. But then I glanced at the clock. Oh. It was only eight o'clock. Oops. She was probably still asleep. The Morelands always slept late on weekends. Embarrassed, I hung up quickly without leaving a message, hoping I hadn't woken anyone up.

I turned back to my room. Ugh. The thought of dealing with it was depressing. But reluctantly, I worked on it until it looked semi-presentable. It would have to do. As I hung Andi's sweater over the chair at my desk, I caught a faint whiff of Crazy About You. I glanced at the clock again. It was now almost nine.

An hour later, I'd finished dusting the living room furniture and had even convinced the twins to take a bath. While Matthew and Jared splashed in the tub I called Andi again—both her line and the family phone. Still no answer, on either line. Hmmm . . . maybe they'd stepped out for breakfast or something.

The morning dragged by. I played with my brothers for a while, and I even gave Basil a bath. Still, Andi didn't call. And when I called her house, there was no answer. Had she forgotten that we were supposed to go ice-skating?

By early afternoon, dread had twisted my stomach into knots. Maybe Andi was mad at *me* because I was bummed that she was going to the dance with Bradley. I wrote a letter on some notebook paper, apologizing for being so weird about it all and rode my bike toward her house to deliver the letter.

The cold wind stung my face, and I had to ride slowly to avoid splashing through the icy puddles. The Morelands' house was quiet, and there were no cars in the driveway. After parking my bike on the driveway, I walked across the lawn to Andi's window. Cold or not, the Morelands loved fresh air, and Andi's window was opened a crack. I folded the note and shoved it through. The curtains were closed, so I couldn't see where it landed.

By the time I got home, a huge storm had started whipping up. The power was off and we had to light the house with battery-powered lights. Mom announced that the phones were dead. Great.

Dinner was dismal. I started to worry about Andi, and even when my dad offered to walk the dog with me, it didn't cheer me up.

Sunday was even worse. The storm continued to rage. Our phones were still out. I was practically jumping out of my skin. Every few minutes, I'd try to call Andi's, but the phone stayed dead. I had just about given up on getting through when it finally rang. I snatched the phone in the living room, but it was only Melissa—the last person in the world I wanted to talk to. She started to babble about some car accident, but I cut her off.

"Can't talk right now," I said, and quickly hung up. Before I could even try Andi, the phone rang again. It was Bradley, of all people. I didn't let him get more than his own name out. "If you're calling to ask me where Andi is, I don't know," I said angrily. "She doesn't tell me anything anymore, thanks to you." I slammed down the receiver.

In about two seconds I realized that I'd sounded like a complete jerk. It wasn't Bradley's fault that Andi hadn't called. I thought about calling him to apologize, but I didn't have his number, and I didn't have the guts to call a guy, anyway.

"Kimmie," my mom said coming into the room just then. "I couldn't help but overhear the way you were talking to one of your friends—"

Just then, the phone rang again. My mom answered it. She wasn't saying anything, and I started to get fidgety. I wondered how I could get her to hang up so I could try Andi again. Then I noticed that her eyes were getting weird, and she started to bite her lip.

"My God, when did this happen?" A pause. "I see. Did they catch the guy?" She nodded, her face turning white.

Something was wrong. Something was terribly wrong. I froze, my breath coming in short little gasps like when I woke up Friday night. I just stood there while my mom murmured things into the phone in a low voice. She hung up, and her eyes filled with tears.

"Somehow, I think you already know," she said to me.

Melissa had started to say something about a car accident. And come to think of it, there was something urgent in Bradley's voice. He'd known something too.

I nodded slowly. "It's Andi. She's been hurt."

"No," Mom choked out. "It's worse than that. Sit down. I don't know how to tell you." She paused, her eyes searching mine. "Andi was killed Friday night. By a drunk driver. She's . . . dead."

Four

"OH, pul-eeze." My voice got thick. I tried to laugh, but it got stuck somewhere in my throat. I just kind of sat there, staring at my mom. She kept looking at me, shaking her head. She started stroking my hair. I pulled back stiffly.

Why was my mom suddenly starting to act all weird? Here she was, telling me that my best friend was dead, when I knew perfectly well it wasn't true. I ask you, how many fifteen-year-olds just go out and die? I don't think so!

"Stop it!" I said in an icy voice. I got up and walked away. My feet moved of their own accord. I walked past the family room where Dad was watching some cartoon video with Matthew and Jared. Out the front door I went. The door never shut completely without giving it a tug, but I didn't bother. I couldn't care less.

For a moment, I just stood perfectly still, not even really aware of the cold air. But then, when I finally started to move, I found that I couldn't take another step. As a matter of fact, I couldn't breathe. I slumped heavily onto the front steps. I heard Basil nudge the door open wider. Then I felt his cold nose under my arm. Mechanically, I stroked his smooth coat.

"Someone's playing a trick on us," I explained to him. He rested his chin on my leg. "It's some sort of a . . . a joke."

That was it! I sat up a little straighter. Of course. Andi was up to something. I'd known her for almost all of my fifteen years. This wasn't the first joke she'd played on me. She'd been pulling them on me since elementary school.

I thought about some of the classics. She'd call me up and not say anything for a few seconds.

"Who's this?" I'd say.

"Pecan," she'd answer in a weird voice.

"Pecan who?" I'd say.

Then Andi's voice: "Pecan someone your own size! Ha ha ha. Didja know it was me?"

"No," I'd answer, even though I did.

Then in middle school. The wild stories she told me about her pets—like the one about her pet turkey attacking some great aunt. Then she'd admit that most of it was made up. A joke. We'd laugh and laugh.

So, fine. This was another one of Andi's jokes. Maybe that's why I tried to laugh when my mom first said, "Andi's dead."

Dead. What a word. And now I was hearing it again. My mom and dad's voices filtered out through the gap in the door behind me. I couldn't hear everything. Maybe because the door wasn't open very far. Maybe because I didn't want to hear what they were saying.

My mom's voice: ". . . a drunk driver . . . Friday night after the movie . . . Mr. and Mrs. Moreland hurt. Alex didn't get a scratch. But Andi . . . Andi didn't make it. The driver was arrested. Drunk."

My dad's voice: "Oh, my God." Silence. Then: "Does Kimmie know?"

Then more silence. Then a roaring in my ears. I stuffed my fingers into my ears to keep their voices out. Basil shoved his nose against me harder, but I pushed him away and put my fingers back in my ears.

Soon, I heard the door squeak. My dad plunked down beside me. He put his arm around me, but didn't say anything. Through the corner of my eye, I watched his breath come out in wispy puffs.

"It's cold out here, punkin," he said after a while. "Let's go in where it's warm."

I shook my head. When I finally spoke, it was like my voice didn't come from me. It was tight and choked. "It's all a joke, you know. Andi does weird stuff like this sometimes, just to get to me. You see, we kinda had this fight, and I think she's mad at me. About this guy named Bradley. I mean, I told her I wasn't mad and all, but you know Andi."

Dad started to say something, but I cut him off.

"Bradley Price. He's this weird, rumply guy who Andi likes. So she can't be dead, because she has this massive crush on him. And she wants to be a news anchor, not a horseshoer, and she has to go to college in order to do that."

I stopped for a second and gulped in some icy cold air. "Anyway . . . anyway, Andi's cheerleading sweater is in my bedroom on my chair. So she has to come get it."

There. That proved it. Andi wasn't dead. I looked at my dad.

"Kimmie, honey. I know this is a terrible

shock, but it's real," he said quietly.

"You don't know what you're talking about," I said, my voice rising. "I know Andi better than anyone in the world, and she'd never do something so horrible to me."

Leaping up, I threw the front door open all the way, then ran up the stairs to my room. First I glanced at the cheerleading sweater over my chair, then I flipped off the light and crawled under my covers. I burrowed all the way down to the end. It was warm and dark and safe, and nothing bad could happen there.

Mom and Dad kept coming in to talk, but I ignored them. Just don't listen to anyone, I told myself. Andi is in her room right now, ready to call and tell me how much she's enjoying her dumb joke.

"What a riot!" she'd say. "Can you believe how flipzoid everyone is acting? Do you believe that they fell for it? Do I sound dead to you?"

"Naw!" I'd yell back. "You sure fooled 'em."

I waited and waited for the phone to ring.

But it didn't.

* * * * *

When I got up the next morning, I realized that sometime during the night I'd thrown off my covers. They were piled on the floor. And I was still in my clothes. Bizarre. Just then, Matthew and Jared came into my room. They had on their Monster Rama pajamas and their hair stuck up. Jared gave me a hug.

"Mom says I'm supposed to give you a hug too," said Matthew. "But I don't want to."

"That's okay," I mumbled. As Jared unlocked his arms from around my neck, Mom came in.

"Hey, sweetie," she said softly, looking like she wasn't sure of what to do.

My dad stepped into the room beside her.

"So what's everyone doing in here?" I demanded. "I've got to get ready for school."

Mom took a deep breath. "Dad and I talked. Maybe you should stay home today. You've had a terrible shock. We all have. Maybe we need a day to just stay home and be together."

"Stay home? It's Monday. Of course I'm going to school."

My mom and dad shot looks at each other.

"I think—" my dad started.

"Wait, Rick," said Mom. "Maybe we should let her go if she wants to." It was her I-Mean-Business voice. Dad let out his breath. He'd caved in.

Just then Matthew pinched Jared, and Jared howled. My mom sighed. "Come on, you guys." She pushed them out my door. Dad followed, after looking back at me a couple of times.

Geez. It was nice to have my room back to myself again! The last thing I needed was to have a family council meeting this morning.

I pulled on my jeans and a white blouse, and topped it off with a woolly green sweater. It took me a while to select earrings, but suddenly it seemed like the most important thing in the world that I had just the right ones on this morning. I kept looking and looking in my jewelry box. Finally, I grabbed a pair of tiny silver hoops.

Downstairs at the breakfast table, no one talked much. Even Matthew and Jared were strangely quiet. Fine by me. I didn't feel like a bunch of noise.

"Well, gotta go," I said as I gulped down the last of my orange juice. Grabbing my books off the counter, I slid them into my book bag and went out the door. I could hear my mom calling my name, but I blocked her out.

The sky was gray again today, but it wasn't as cold as before. Good thing. I'd forgotten my stupid jacket. When I got to school, I stood there looking at the brick building for a while. Of course I'd seen it a zillion times before, but today it looked . . . different. Unwelcoming. And the inside of the building looked as gray as the outside. I started wishing that maybe I'd listened to my mom and dad and stayed home.

A couple of students looked at me like I was an alien from another planet. And then the two mean Miss Populars of our school, Melissa Hendricks and Amy Lynn Pritchard, spotted me and came over, wide-eyed. Interested.

"Isn't it awful?" they said to me. But their eyes seemed to say, "Tell us more."

"Isn't what awful?" I shot back, looking them both right in those glinty eyes.

"You know . . . about Andrea," said Amy.

"What about Andrea? Her name's Andi," I almost yelled.

Two other kids walking by stared at me. I jerked my chin up at them and clutched the straps of my book bag, toying with them nervously.

"Oh, come on. I called you last night to see what you knew," said Melissa. "And it was in the newspaper. Some drunk old man on Friday night. It happened on Fifth Street. Everybody's talking about it."

I folded my arms across my chest, daring another word.

Melissa glanced at Amy, then said to me, "You must know. Everyone figured your family would be the first to hear about the car accident. And that Andi is . . . dead." She started fiddling with the zipper on her book bag.

"You think you know everything just because . . . because you're a cheerleader," I yelled. "Well, you don't. You don't know anything! Don't you ever, EVER say that about Andi!"

I spun around and bolted down the hallway, pushing past clusters of students. I felt like something horrible was trying to get me. I ran past the science labs, down the stairs, and around a corner, where I proceeded to smash full on into Bradley Price. The last guy on earth I wanted to see, let alone smash into. I knew his eyes would have that same look as Melissa's and Amy's. Full of questions. Maybe a gushy look of concern thrown in for good measure. I couldn't stand it. I couldn't. I kept my eyes locked on his blue denim jacket so I didn't have to see his face.

"Kimmie," he said in a low voice. He stepped back. I shot past him and tore blindly into the girls' restroom. I locked myself inside a stall and sank onto the cool tile floor and leaned against the door.

"Kimmie, are you in there?" came a girl's voice I didn't recognize. I heard footsteps come up to the stall, pause, then stride away, out the door.

Fine. I wanted to be alone. People were getting weird all around me.

"They're lying," I said, hugging my knees. My voice echoed around the empty restroom. "They're lying," I said again. I said it about thirty times. Each time I said it louder and louder, until new footsteps announced the arrival of someone else.

"Kimmie? Kimmie Bowen. It's Mrs. Baldwin."

Who? It took a while for the name to register. It was the school nurse. She tapped the metal door behind me. Slowly, I stood and picked up my book bag, then turned around and opened the door.

"I'm not sick," I said when I saw her.

"Of course you're not," she said.

Just then, I let out this choked sob and I fell forward into her thick arms.

She gently led me to the infirmary and made me lie down on a cot covered with a scratchy blanket. "I'm not sick," I repeated. But tears kept getting in the way of my voice.

It was only when Mom came through the door that I could stand up and talk again.

"Take me home," I said shakily. "I think you were right. I don't think I should be at school."

What I wanted to say, but didn't, was that I wanted to slip over to Andi's house and tell her about my awful morning, and could she even believe what jerks Melissa and Amy were to say such a weird thing about her?

As Mom drove me home she talked soothingly in words that I couldn't quite catch. Then she eased me up the stairs and brought me a tall glass of cold chocolate milk. My favorite, and Andi's. No, better not think about that.

I sat on a wicker chair next to my stereo

and tried not to think. In fact, that's how I mostly spent the next two days. Eating meals and not thinking. Reading books and not thinking. Scratching Basil behind his ears and not thinking. Occasionally putting up with visits from the Human Whirlwinds, Matthew and Jared. Listening to Mom ask me if I felt up to going to the funeral . . . and not thinking.

"Okay," I said. "I'll go." But only because I knew that finally Andi would have to come and tell everyone it was just a huge joke. That she really was alive, and then she'd come over to my house again and everything would be like it was. We'd borrow each other's clothes and visit Mrs. L at Pet City and discuss guinea pigs. And gossip about people. And figure out what to do about Bradley, since really, the last thing Andi needed was a boyfriend.

There was too much stuff we had left to do together.

Five

THE next day, I woke up slowly. I had a feeling that something important was supposed to happen, but I didn't really want to know what it was. But then my brain cleared and it hit me. Today was the funeral. Andi's funeral.

Today I would be going to a funeral for my best friend.

I put on the dark green dress I usually reserved for church and spritzed on some Crazy About You perfume. As I sat quietly in my room, just waiting, I could hear breakfast being served below in the kitchen. Jared's voice rose in a whine. We were out of his favorite cereal. Then I heard a car pull up our driveway. Aimlessly, I got up to see who it was. Aunt Catherine. Mom's sister. My favorite aunt. A few minutes later she came to my room and knocked lightly.

"Come in," I said listlessly.

She was carrying a breakfast tray. "Your parents sent me on a mission to bring you this. They're getting the twins ready. I'm taking them for the day," she explained. She set the tray on my desk, then sat on my bed while I nibbled toast and sipped orange juice.

Aunt Catherine, I thought, studying her. She was a pediatrician in the next town, and a very efficient type. When I was younger she attended all my T-ball games, and a few times I saw her in action when one of the girls got hurt. She would calmly put splints on fingers and legs, talking all the while to the injured kid. For a while, Andi and I thought we wanted to be pediatricians like Aunt Catherine.

"I'm sorry about what you're having to go through," she said now. "It's never easy to lose someone you love. I was lost when your Uncle Randy died. But somehow, you learn to go on."

I nodded because I knew it was expected. She mumbled some other stuff about living and dying. I didn't want to listen, so instead, I concentrated on chewing my toast. If I really tried, I could get in about eighteen chews before I had to swallow.

Finally, Aunt Catherine stood and hugged me, then went downstairs. After a while, I heard the sounds of Matthew and Jared being loaded into the car. Then the car started up and purred down the driveway.

My parents came into my room. My dad squeezed my shoulder and said, "I wish I knew what to say. Are you okay, kiddo?"

Okay? How could I be okay—how could anything be okay again?

My mom looked at him.

"Geez," I complained. "Why does everyone keep looking at everyone. Why don't they just say what's on their minds?"

Mom and Dad looked at each other again, then laughed nervously. I didn't get it. Any of it. I turned away.

And then it was time. We got into our car. As we drove slowly to church, I looked out the car window. I peered at each house that we passed. There were whole families inside. They were important to each other. They had friends. They would be going on errands today, maybe getting together with each other.

They weren't going to funerals.

We parked in the lot by our big brick church. There was a long white car parked in front of us. All around us, people were getting out of their cars. Melissa Hendricks waved at me, as if she was glad to see me. I turned away. Why was she suddenly being so nice? She'd never really had the time of day for me before.

Shannon and Charley had come with Shannon's mom and dad. I spotted Amy and some other kids from school, plus a bunch of people I'd seen at Andi's house before. Friends of her parents. Even Ms. Sharp was here, the teacher Andi wanted to beam off the face of Planet Earth. And there was Bradley. I turned my back to him.

Everywhere I looked, there were too many people wearing church clothes and looking like they really didn't belong in them. Well, of course not; it was Thursday, not Sunday.

As I walked up the church steps with my mom and dad holding each of my hands, I thought about the Sunday School years when Andi and I had walked through these doors. We'd been here a zillion times. And now we were here again.

Old Mrs. Alcroft was playing the organ. Andi used to imitate Mrs. Alcroft when we were younger. When no one was looking she would sneak over to the organ and sit down in a big, show-off way. She'd beam like Mrs. Alcroft did and play "Chopsticks" with an exaggerated flourish. If she heard the slow, haunting melody Mrs. Alcroft was playing now, she would make faces at me. "Pu—leeze," she would say. "Can you stand this noise? Let's get Rae Ann in here and show her what real music is!"

I sat in a pew a few rows back from Andi's parents. I studied their backs while the minister said nice things about some stranger named Andrea Moreland. My eyes stayed fixed on a glass-framed picture of Andi near the flower-covered casket.

Geez. Andi hated that picture. It was taken last fall, and she complained that she was having a Bad Hair Day. She wanted to have it taken again. Of course, she'd forgotten to show up for picture make-up day, so then she was stuck with the weird picture. She'd be bummed, knowing that Bradley Price was at that very minute looking at it.

I looked around to where Bradley sat. He was staring at the stained glass windows. My gaze followed his. I squinted so that the colored glass fuzzed. The way the colors and lights blurred reminded me of the sunlight playing off the water at the California beach that Andi and I had visited together a couple of years ago. A cousin of hers lived at Newport Beach. I'd gotten to fly to California with her family, see Disneyland, and play at the beach for a week. We'd taken her cousin's clunky old bicycles and had ridden up and down the boardwalk. Andi had named her bike "Seahorse" and talked to it as if it were real. Later, we sat on the pier with our legs dangling off the edge and watched the sunlight playing on the water. We talked about Big Important Things.

I closed my eyes and listened to the music. If I kept my eyes shut tightly, maybe the tears wouldn't squeeze out.

The joke's gone too far, I murmured to myself. It was time for Andi to walk into the church and apologize for scaring everyone and making them wear church clothes on a Thursday, and for making them think she was dead.

"I'm sorry. My joke got out of hand," she would say, gazing at all of us sitting there looking so serious. Everyone would shake their heads at her and get up to leave, to get on with their regular Thursday things. After all, they really didn't belong here on a weekday.

I waited all through the service, but no Andi.

Afterward, everyone stood around on the church steps. My mom and dad shook hands with Mr. and Mrs. Moreland. As I looked at their exhausted faces, I wondered if they would ever feel like laughing again. I knew I wouldn't. Alex, Andi's big brother, stood next to them, with his hands shoved into the pockets of his gray suit pants. He must have grown since his parents bought the suit. The pants were too short, exposing dark socks that trailed into his shoes.

"Hey, Kimmie," Alex said. He hugged me. He smelled of aftershave and strong soap. He looked older, somehow. Like overnight, he'd gone from being a high school guy I knew to a total grownup. It scared me.

I mumbled something to Alex, then eased into the crowd, watching the people around me. I really didn't belong here. I belonged at school. Andi and I would be at our lockers about now. Squeezing my eyes, I tried to shut out everything around me.

"Kimmie." It was Bradley's voice.

Reluctantly, I opened my eyes and looked at him. Andi's almost-boyfriend. He was carrying a bouquet of flowers wrapped in clear plastic. He looked nervous in his navy blazer and gray pants. Not like a rumpled grocery bag at all. He looked . . . well, starched and folded. He twisted the end of the plastic around and around.

"She would have liked . . . what the minister said about her," he mumbled.

I looked down and saw that Bradley's shoe was untied. I wondered how Andi could like someone who couldn't keep his shoes tied and who brought her flowers with the plastic still wrapped around them. Then it occurred to me that she'd like flowers that Bradley brought her even if they were wrapped in old newspapers. And that thought made me laugh. Which then made me cry.

Next thing, my dad was there, and he pulled me close to his side. I traced the pattern of his pinstripes with my fingertip. The lines went up and down like they were supposed to, and everything made sense.

Bradley shuffled away, and Dad and I watched as the Morelands climbed into a white limousine. It followed another white limousine that was filled with flowers. They were pink and yellow and cheery, not like the gray sky. Iowa was always so gray, I thought to myself, watching the long car.

Maybe if I moved to California or Hawaii when I grew up, I wouldn't have to see gray days ever again.

My dad led me to our car, and Mom joined us there. Then we drove behind the white car filled with flowers until it brought us to the cemetery.

Everyone sort of clung together. I stood behind the others by myself. My eyes swept over the greenish-brown grass. There were granite stones everywhere. Soon, there would be one with Andi's name on it. I looked up at the sky. It was easier not to have to look at Andi's casket. I could pretend she wasn't really inside it.

The whole thing was ridiculous. All these sad-faced people. All these flowers. No Andi. Just everybody in the whole world who knew Andi.

* * * * *

That night, I watched TV for hours. I clicked the remote control every few seconds. Jagged images of a thousand things flashed across the screen. Shiny new cars. Jungle creatures. Newscasters. Sitcom families in picture-perfect kitchens. Commercials for tooth polishes and headache tablets. People were smiling to show off their shiny white teeth, and they were smiling when their headaches were gone. Laughing with their friends and families.

None of them had anything to do with my life, so I zapped the images and kept waiting for one that was going to give me some idea of what I was going to do now—now that Andi was gone.

Six

FRIDAY felt normal. Too normal. I got up and showered and went about putting myself together for school as always. My eyes looked puffy, but I ignored them. I spent a long time in the bathroom blow-drying my hair and curling it with a curling iron. Like it mattered. When I was finally dressed, I went down to help Mom with the boys. But today Mom wasn't wearing a suit. She had on a comfy old Iowa Hawkeyes sweatshirt and jeans.

"I brought the computer home, so I can work here," she announced when she saw my look. "I'll take Matthew and Jared to daycare, then take you to school and pick you up this afternoon."

Mom hardly ever took time off work. My first thought was that she felt sorry for me because of Andi. Well, if staying home made her feel better, fine. I really didn't have the energy to tell her that she didn't have to.

In the car on the way to school, Mom asked me a string of questions about my subjects and teachers. I gave her one-word answers. All of that seemed so far away. I didn't see what it had to do with anything.

"Are you all right, punkin?" Mom asked as we drew close to the school. "Should I be worried about you?"

I shrugged. I mean, what did she think? Really. But then, as we turned into the parking lot in front of school, my eyes started to burn. There were kids everywhere. Some were standing together in groups. A few were talking and laughing. Others were sitting on the low walls, studying. One girl with curly long blond hair whizzed by our car on her bike. Not one of those kids was Andi. Uh-oh, I was about to cry again.

Quickly, I willed the tears away. I was tired of crying. Mom said I could call anytime if I needed to and she'd be there.

I headed to my locker and just kind of stood there for a minute. Maybe, I thought as I spun the combination, there would be a rat in it or some other joke.

No. Just my books. And Andi's. I stood

there looking at them for a while. So, what was I supposed to do with them? And what about the animal posters that she had plastered on the inside of the door? It hurt to try to figure it out, so I just grabbed a couple of my books and slammed the locker door shut.

"Hullo, Kimmie." I turned around. It was Bradley. He was wearing a Hawkeyes sweatshirt today too. What was this with the sporty look, I wondered.

"You okay?" he asked. When I didn't answer, he looked embarrassed, then turned to open his locker. I watched him.

"Why do people keep asking me if I'm okay?" I finally blurted out.

Bradley rummaged in his locker, his back to me. Then he pushed back his boring brown hair and shoved his hands into his jeans pockets. "So what else are they supposed to ask?" he asked harshly. In the next instant, he softened and shrugged. "Maybe it's because no one knows what to say."

I considered that for a sec. Then I nodded and adjusted my books. "Yeah," I agreed. "You're probably right. There just isn't anything to say."

"The whole thing stinks," Bradley burst

out. "Andi's a nice kid. It's not fair. She doesn't deserve to have some guy who chugged too many beers take her life away."

I nodded and started off down the hall, realizing as I walked that Bradley spoke of Andi in the present tense, not in the past. Not like everyone else I'd been listening to for the past few days. The older people, the Morelands' friends, said stuff like, "Andi was such a lovely girl." Or, "I never knew someone who was so full of life."

Pu-leeze. I liked it that Bradley said, "Andi is." It made it feel like Andi was still here, walking down the hall with me, maybe talking about her algebra quiz. I bet her grade was still there in Ms. Sharp's grade book.

That gave me an idea. I walked over to Room 210. Good. Ms. Sharp was there, sitting in front of the classroom, checking some papers. She had two or three students there, probably making up a test or getting help on homework.

She looked up when I entered. "Um, Ms. Sharp, could I ask you something?" I said.

"What can I do for you, Kimberly?" Ms. Sharp put down her pencil and folded her hands on her desk.

"Maybe you think it's none of my business, but I . . ." My voice got caught in my throat. I took a deep breath and tried again. "I helped Andi study for her quiz, and I wonder how she did."

Ms. Sharp studied my face as if deciding what to do. Finally, she nodded. "Well, it's against school policy to tell one student another student's grade. But I can tell you that she did surprisingly well. I had wondered who helped her, and now I know. You did a good job tutoring her."

I ducked my head and mumbled a thanks. I don't know why, but I needed to know.

"You did it, Andi," I whispered to no one in the hallway. "Keep it up, and you won't lose your cheerleading spot." Suddenly, I felt like I'd been kicked in the stomach. So I made myself stop thinking and I managed to get through the day. A few kids looked at me weird. Shannon and Charley chose me to be on their basketball team in P.E., and we beat Melissa and Amy's team. None of it mattered, though. Because Andi wasn't there to giggle with me afterward about our triumph.

During lunch, I ate in the corner of the cafeteria, away from everyone. I just couldn't deal with people right now. Every so often, I'd hear a familiar laugh and look up, half-expecting Andi to sort of walk into the cafeteria.

Mom and Jared and Matthew came to pick me up after school.

"Matthew pushed a girl today, and he had to go sit on the unfriendly bench," Jared said to me gleefully when I slid onto the seat and closed the door.

"That wasn't very nice," I said automatically. Matthew was always getting into trouble.

"She pushed me," Matthew grumbled. "I hate her, so I pushed her."

"Matthew, we already went over this," Mom said wearily as she pulled out of the school driveway. "We've got to make a stop at the grocery store, so you two behave yourselves."

I slid down in my seat. Ugh. I didn't want to go anywhere where people we know might bump into us and give us those looks and ask me if I was okay. I scowled, wondering why Mom hadn't just gone to the store while I was at school.

We passed Pet City on the way. I glanced in the window as we drove by and spotted Mrs. L at the cash register. Did she wonder why Andi hadn't been in for a few days, or did she know? I slumped further in my seat.

That evening, after I did my history homework, I automatically picked up the phone. Halfway through punching in Andi's number, I remembered that she wouldn't be answering anymore. But for some reason, I finished punching in her number. The phone rang four times before her answering machine came on: "Hello. You have reached Andi's animal house. I can't come to the phone right now, so too bad, so sad. Leave your name and all that stuff, and I'll call back." Then I heard the sounds of her animals in the background and a beep. I hung up.

Something made me call again. And again. Listening to Andi's voice, I felt an ache that began deep in my stomach. Each time I hung up without leaving a message. Andi's voice. It sounded just like she was at the other end of the phone. Finally, I punched the number and left a message: "Hi. It's me, Kimmie. Andi . . . I miss you." I hung up quickly.

"Kimmie, that was dumb," I lectured myself.

My brothers came jamming into my room just then.

"You're supposed to knock first," I grumbled.

"You're no fun. I wish Andi would come

over here," Jared said with a pout.

"She can't. She's dead." That came from Matthew. He promptly knocked over some books on my desk and sent my lamp tumbling headfirst onto my carpet.

"Shut up! Get out of here," I snapped, reaching over to scoop up my books.

They didn't. Matthew chased Jared around my room while I yelled at them. Hearing the noise, Dad thundered in. Then he ordered the boys out of my room and gently asked me to ease up. A little while later I could hear the sounds of Dad putting Matthew and Jared to bed.

I collapsed on my bed and closed my eyes. I imagined that Andi was coming through my door. I could see her clearly, those laughing eyes and dark hair that she could never get to curl right. She would be wearing her ever-present cheerleader sweater, and would say, "Hey, what's up? Why are you just sitting there? Come on. We've got stuff to do!" Then we'd turn up my stereo full blast. We'd laugh and talk about things, and plan for the weekend—and maybe the weekend after that.

Only now the weekends stretched endlessly ahead, and there was no one to help me figure out what to do with all of them.

Seven

IT was weird. Over the next few weeks, things started appearing on my bed. Magazine articles like "Living With Loss." Little notes from Aunt Catherine: "Read this, honey." She would highlight sentences in bright yellow marker.

Once I found a little book of quotations. Someone had turned down the corners on pages that had quotes like "It's better to have loved and lost than never to have loved at all." There was one book about death written especially for teens. I thumbed through it briefly. "Getting over the loss of a loved one isn't an accident," I read. "It's a deliberate action." My eyes scanned the words, but my heart refused to take them in. Oh, pul-eeze, Andi would say.

Every day was just a repeat of the day before. I dragged myself out of bed. Went to school on the weekdays, hung around the house on the weekend. I never did so much homework. It was as if each homework assignment was the most important thing in the world. I'd stay up late in the evenings, carefully writing and rewriting my essays, copying over my math assignments so there would be no erasures.

On Saturdays, I would wait for the mailman, then rush out to grab the mail, as if I were expecting something interesting. The most interesting thing I got was a postcard from Grandpa Pete.

One Friday morning, I headed downstairs after dressing for school. Jared was singing at the breakfast table while Matthew ran around the kitchen making wailing noises like a siren. I clapped my hands over my ears. "Stop it, you guys. You're supposed to be eating your breakfast," I shouted above the din.

"You're always yelling at us," complained Jared. He glared at me, then dropped a glob of cereal on the floor. Basil promptly lumbered over to slurp it up. Then he burped. Gross!

Without stopping for breakfast or saying goodbye to my parents or anything, I tore out of the house and ran all the way to school. It seemed better to sit outside on the low brick wall alone than to stay inside my house with my brothers, who never backed off, never gave me a chance.

The next morning, I was hit with a numbing depression. I couldn't get dressed and run to the safety of an organized school day. I had the prospect of a whole dismal weekend ahead of me. The last couple of weekends had been the pits. I'd stayed in my room and thought about the weeks stretching ahead of me. Lonely weeks at school, then lonely weekends at home. But this weekend was different. It bothered me that I had nowhere to go and nothing planned.

"What can I do today?" I asked my mom later that morning while she and Dad puttered around, straightening up the house.

She suggested the mall. My dad even said he'd drive me there if I felt like going alone.

"Why would I want to go there?" I said to Mom.

"You'd mentioned a while back that you needed a new school outfit or two. You could go and pick out something nice."

"No, thanks."

Mom looked hurt. So did my dad. But

didn't they understand? What was the point of shopping if I had to go without Andi? There would be no one to tell me if the outfit I tried on was totally stupid or to die for. No one to tell me just the perfect belt or socks to go with it. No one to eat corn dogs with at the food court afterward.

I tromped upstairs and called Andi's answering machine. For the first few days after the funeral, I left her a message every day. Sometimes two times a day. Then I stopped because I knew it must be a dumb thing to do, and it didn't change anything. But today I wanted to connect again. I didn't care what it seemed like. I punched in Andi's number and listened to the phone ringing on the other end, planning what I would say: "Andi, I'm bored, bored, bored. What should I do today? I need some ideas." But this time the phone just rang and rang. Someone had disconnected the answering machine. Quietly, I hung up. I felt like I had lost Andi all over again.

The weekend dragged on. Other than going with my family to my cousin's fifth birthday party and watching all the little kids go flipzoid, I stayed in my room. By Sunday afternoon, I wondered if this was the way it would be for the rest of my life.

Would I just sit around? Go places with my dweezoid little brothers?

Gazing out the living room window, I studied the brown, slushy snow sitting on the ground. It would be cold and blah outside, but I had to get out of the house. I'd spent too much time in here lately. I ran up to my room and put on tights under my jeans, a warm navy sweater, and my ski jacket.

Once outside, I took a gulp of icy air. It made my eyes sting and my chest hurt, but I didn't care. I was outside, away from the house. I started walking down the street, not caring where I was going. As I walked, I got used to the cold air. I listened to the sound my feet made as they crunched in the icy, dirty snow.

When I got to the street corner, I stopped and watched a few cars whiz by. Funny. Those people all had places to go, and I had nowhere. I stepped out onto the street to cross, and was halfway to the other side when a car turned right and crossed right in front of me. I jumped back, feeling the blast of wind where the car had been.

"Watch where you're going, nerd breath!" I yelled at the fast-disappearing car. My heart thudded. I could have been killed, just like that—suddenly, and without warning. Like Andi. I started to think about the freshman dance, and how now it was to be sponsored by a newly formed club of Students Standing Up Against Drunk Driving.

"We won't stand for it," Melissa Hendricks had proclaimed dramatically at an assembly last week. She had been elected president of the students' group. They'd shown a film about drinking and driving. I closed my eyes through the whole thing, but the message wasn't lost on me. Drunk drivers had senselessly plowed down a lot of people. Nice people like Andi, and others—mothers, fathers, someone's boyfriend or girlfriend. Best friends.

I started walking faster. "It's not fair. It's not fair," I chanted silently with each step. After a while, I looked up and realized I was on Andi's street. I did an abrupt about-face and started walking quickly in the opposite direction, toward my own house. What if I walked by her house and it wasn't there anymore?

At home once again, I flopped on the rug in our family room and stared at the blank TV screen. Before long, my mom came in.

"Kimmie?" She sat on the rug next to me. "How are you?"

"Mad," I said simply. It didn't make sense. I knew it. But that's what I was. My mother probably thought I was weirding out all over the place.

To my surprise, she nodded her head. "I figured you'd probably be mad."

I sat up. "You did? But it's dumb, huh? It's not like Andi wanted this."

"I know. And you're angry. You're angry that something like this had to happen to someone you loved."

I looked at the floor. "Yeah. Mostly that. But I'm also mad at her . . . because she left me behind." I felt guilty, and I wanted to shut up, but I couldn't. "What am I supposed to do by myself all the time? What did Andi think? That I would enjoy sitting alone in the cafeteria? That I would like walking home by myself?"

My voice started climbing higher and higher. Then it ended in a choked sob. The floodgates burst open, and I started crying in torrents. Big, huge tears.

My mom hugged me tightly. "You know, honey, Aunt Catherine was telling me that there are grief recovery groups for teens. You could go and sit with people your age and talk about some of the things you're feeling," she ventured.

I sobbed harder. The idea of talking about people you'd loved and lost with perfect strangers—even if they were my age—was too much. I couldn't talk about it now. I couldn't even think about it.

Oh, Andi, how could you go away? I sobbed. How could you make it forever and ever?

Eight

WHEN I got home from school Monday afternoon, I found a message for me on our answering machine.

"Hi, this is Aunt Catherine. I'm calling for Kimmie. I'm stopping by after my hospital rounds this evening to pick you up. Let's go to the Blueberry Inn for dinner. See you at 6:30."

When Mom came home with the boys, I told her about Aunt Catherine's message.

"We want to go too," Matthew and Jared clamored.

Mom quickly shushed them and told them the invitation was extended to me only. I didn't feel like dressing up, but Mom wouldn't hear of my not going. By the time Aunt Catherine showed up at our door, I was dressed in my good pants and a soft white sweater.

She was wearing a coral suit with a gold pin shaped like a leaf. She smelled like rubbing alcohol, but her smile was warm. Suddenly I was glad to be going with her.

The restaurant was cozy, and when we were seated, Aunt Catherine told me to order anything I wanted. My eyes scanned the menu, looking for something appealing. I hadn't felt like eating much lately. My clothes were starting to get sort of loose. Finally I settled on broiled chicken with potatoes and a salad.

While we waited for our food, Aunt Catherine gently asked about school. Then she told me some stories about her young patients. She talked about some kid named Jason who terrorized the pediatrics ward with a new remote-controlled monster truck someone brought him. It was obvious that Aunt Catherine had a soft spot for this kid. I listened but didn't say much. She didn't ask me once if I was okay. Right in the middle of my dessert of chocolate chip cheesecake, I brought up the subject of Andi. I wasn't planning to. It just slipped out.

"You miss her so much," she said softly.

"I can't seem to think of anything else," I confessed, my voice getting tight.

Aunt Catherine nodded and waited for me to continue.

"I did read some of those articles you left for me," I said, because I knew it would make her feel better.

Still Aunt Catherine said nothing. She stirred her coffee and the spoon clinked against the cup.

"And my mom mentioned something about those grief sessions teens can go to," I added. I gulped. "Thing is, I can't just go and do what the books all say, or talk about it with people I don't know. But I do want a normal life again. Are there people who just . . . don't get over this?"

Hearing the words aloud suddenly terrified me. It made them seem so real. Was it possible that I could live my whole life and never fill the dark hole Andi's death had left?

Aunt Catherine put her hand on my arm. "Everyone comes to terms with death in his or her own way, on an individual timetable. You can't just sit there and wait for life to let you back in. You have to roll up your sleeves and get in there again.

"How?" I asked.

Aunt Catherine pursed her lips while she thought. "It's not like there's any one formula for everybody. There is no 'one size fits all.' But maybe there's a way to start.

For instance, do you have any hobbies?"

My face must have looked blank, because she rushed on. "Like drawing or painting or writing poetry?"

Did I have any hobbies? Did doing homework count? Everything I used to do was because of Andi.

"Do you belong to any clubs at school?" Aunt Catherine asked.

I shook my head. I'd gone ice-skating with Andi at times, but it wasn't what you'd call a hobby. Big deal. Zipping around on a crowded ice rink. I'd wanted to join the drama club once, but Andi had hated it. And since I had this thing about getting up in front of people, it was easy enough to give in to her.

Cheerleading . . . well, that was really more Andi's thing. So were animals. I mean, Basil's okay, but I could never get into pets the way Andi had. No, if I had a hobby at all, it was Andi and doing whatever she was doing.

I took a bite of my cheesecake, half-wondering how the Blueberry Inn bakers made it, and half-thinking about how I had no real hobbies. Except . . . wait. A long time ago, I used to hang around in the kitchen and ask my mom if I could bake things. I'd made fudge that tasted so good that my dad polished it off in one day. And I'd made a cinnamon coffee cake that my mom served to some people who worked with her. They said it was the most delicious cake they had ever eaten.

"I like—that is, I used to bake," I heard myself saying.

"That's a start," said Aunt Catherine, signaling for the bill as if that was settled.

So that was why a few days later, I was baking mini chocolate chip muffins when our doorbell rang. I didn't feel like answering it, so I just stayed by the oven, watching through the glass. If I'd done everything right, the muffins should be rising just about now.

The bell rang again.

"Kimmie, would you get that please? I've got Matthew and Jared in the bathtub." My mom's voice sailed down the stairs.

I sighed and wiped my hands on a dish towel, then headed for the door and pulled it open.

Shannon and Charley were there, stamping their feet in the cold. "Hi," Shannon said. "Charley and I were just hanging around, and we wondered if, well, maybe you wanted to do something."

I wondered if I looked as surprised as I felt. Shannon and Charley and I hadn't hung around together in like forever. I almost said no, thanks, I had stuff to do. But then another voice inside said, "Right, Kimmie. What do you have to do?"

I smiled. "Sure. Come on in. I'm baking chocolate chip muffins."

"Yum," said Charley, sniffing the air as we went into the kitchen. "I didn't know you baked."

"I don't usually," I confessed. "It's just that I was bored, and the twins started yapping about muffins, and I thought, oh, why not?"

Charley and Shannon sort of stood there. I didn't know what to do. It was weird. I wasn't really used to having new people over. I was only used to having Andi over, and we just did things the same way we always did. But then I thought about what Mrs. Moreland would do. She'd offer you something to eat and drink and tell you to have a seat.

So that's what I did. I got the muffins out of the oven and the three of us sat around the kitchen table and started wolfing them down with hot chocolate. Of course, the minute we sat down, Jared and

Matthew flew in, hot and pink from the tub, demanding muffins. I gave them each a couple. Then, luckily, they decided they wanted to go destroy something in the family room.

"Twins are so cute," said Charley, watching them go.

I made a face. "Sometimes. But most of the time, they're a double pain. When one's asleep, the other's awake. And we're always having to keep them from killing themselves."

"I can't tell one from the other!" Shannon said. "How do you know which one's which?"

People always asked that.

"It's easy enough." I explained. "Matthew's hair sticks up more than Jared's. And Matthew's much more like this . . . turbo kid. Jared's the quieter of the two, although sometimes it's hard to tell."

From there, our conversation turned to school. For a while, we talked about the homework that was piling up on us. Then Shannon brought up the freshman dance. Geez. It was coming up soon.

"Melissa and Amy talked us into helping out," Charley said. "I guess that . . . because of what happened, we should all pitch in to help raise money for the kids who are putting up a fight against drunk drivers."

They both looked at me. Oh. So that was it. Melissa had probably sent them over to try to talk me into doing some work for the dance because there was no way she'd come over herself. She knew that I basically couldn't stand her. But why would she want me to work with her? She probably had tons of people on all her committees. I sipped my hot chocolate and looked at the linoleum floor. "I suppose you think I'm awful, but I . . . I just can't."

How could I explain the way I felt? I mean, even before The Thing happened with Andi, I'd had some pretty weird feelings about the dance anyway. If I helped out with it, I'd have to go, and Andi wouldn't be there and—no. The whole scenario was too much for me.

"It's for a good cause." Shannon was trying again. "The Students Standing Up Against Drunk Driving could use everyone's support. You, more than a lot of people, should know that."

There was a silence. Charley finally spoke again. "Melissa asked me to ask you if you'd give a dedication at the dance to Andi."

Me in front of all those kids at Riverview High School? A bunch of glinty-eyed kids wanting me to tell them the details about what happened to Andi? A lot of the kids didn't even know her.

Oh, Andi, I thought. I need your help. Get me out of this mess!

I felt my eyes start to swim. Charley got up and awkwardly patted my shoulder. "Everyone at school's wondering about you, Kimmie. People are waiting to see what you think about all of this. It would mean a lot to everyone at school if you'd be part of it."

Me? Why? I was boring Kimmie Lee Bowen. I was practically invisible at school. I wasn't a cheerleader, the student organizer type. I wasn't Miss Friends-With-Everyone. That had been Andi's job. Just because Andi wasn't here didn't mean that I was going to step into her shoes. I didn't know how.

"Just let people know that I . . . I can't," I said thickly. I studied the bottom of my empty cup. "I'm not . . . like Andi. I can't talk and have a whole roomful of people listen to me. Anyway, I wouldn't know what to say."

Charley's eyes grew wide. "I'd think you'd have a lot to say. You were Andi's best friend, and you knew her better than anyone at our whole school."

"Besides, you're a good English student, and everyone thought you gave a great speech last year when you ran for eighth-grade student government," Shannon chimed in.

That was only because Andi talked me into running for vice president since she was running for president. And because she supplied all the funny lines. Yeah, we both got elected, but I never would have had the nerve to even try if it hadn't been for Andi. But I didn't say any of that.

"I can't," I said lamely.

"But—" Shannon started. She darted a look at Charley and her jaw slapped shut.

"We should go," Charley said quietly.

After I walked them to the door, I returned to the kitchen to clean up the muffin mess. Ugh. My stomach felt blah. I wondered if I should have just given in.

Oh, who knows anything anymore, I thought irritably. I went up to my room. My homework was piled on my desk, but I didn't even bother trying to do it. Basil nudged open my door and ambled over. I flopped on my bed and stared at the ceiling and scratched Basil behind his ears.

He licked my hand.

Maybe that's why Andi liked animals so much, I thought. They didn't ask a lot from anyone.

* * * * *

The next morning, I got a surprise. My Western Civ teacher, Mr. Blake, handed me a Warning Report.

"I know things have been hard for you lately," he said gently after class. "Your homework is well-prepared, but your classwork is suffering. Your grade's slipping . . . and I just thought you should know. I don't expect an instant turnaround, but it's something you might want to put your mind to."

"I'll try harder," I said quietly, putting the Warning Report in my notebook.

"You know, if you need to talk, I'm always here," he said.

After mumbling a thank you, I slipped out the door. I walked down the hall, my eyes to the floor and my mood plunging. But maybe Mr. Blake had a point, I thought as I headed to my next class. Maybe I should throw myself into my studies.

At lunch I ate quickly, then hurried to the library and ducked inside. I selected a table near the back and opened my books. For a while, I reviewed my Spanish notes, but soon I was bored. I walked up and down the aisles, and finally I found myself in the fiction section. I hadn't read a good book in a while. Maybe it was just the thing I needed. I could lose myself in a story.

I selected a mystery and had just returned to my seat when I heard a pair of heavy footsteps. Looking up, I saw Bradley Price heading toward me. He nodded and plopped his book bag next to mine.

"Hi," he said. "Is anyone else sitting here?"

I didn't answer, but started to scan the book jacket. Bradley sat down. I hoped he wouldn't start talking to me. He'd probably try to talk me into doing the dedication at the dance. But he didn't. He flipped open his math book and pulled his calculator out of his book bag.

I peeked at him for a sec. He was wearing a thick navy sweater, and his hair in back kind of curled down over his sweater. He needs a haircut, I thought. But my eyes kept returning to where his hair curled down over his sweater. I went back to reading the back of the book jacket, but part of me was thinking that having Bradley sitting there doing his math next to me was . . . well, comforting. Kinda like having Basil nearby when I was doing my homework at home.

It was warm and quiet in the library, and I could hear rain start rapping against the window. Then I opened the book. Inside was the card that you fill out when you want to check out a book. The last person to have checked out "The Mystery at Kilford Crossing" was . . . Andrea Moreland. I recognized her weird, tiny handwriting instantly. The ink on the *A* had smudged. I set the book down heavily. Bradley looked up and he switched off his calculator.

"I miss her too," he said quietly.

And so we just sat there, missing her. And we sat there missing her for the next few days at lunch hour too. Not really talking, just sitting and waiting.

* * * * *

Two days before the freshman dance, someone called my mom. I was in the kitchen, thumbing through a cookbook. I could hear my mom on the family room phone saying, "No. It's just not something she wants to do at this time. Yes. Yes, I'm sure."

She hung up and came into the kitchen. "The school principal. She was just checking one last time to see if there was any way you'd reconsider and do the dedication for the dance. I told her that you just weren't up to it." Her eyes scanned mine. "Was I right?"

"Geez," I complained. "Everyone's in on this campaign. No one ever cared what I had to say before."

Mom ruffled my hair. "It's not exactly like that. But anyway, if that's what you've decided, I'll stand by you."

I wandered up to my room and tried to picture myself standing in front of a group of kids. Talking about Andi. I shook my head. I couldn't do it. No way.

Aimlessly, I started doodling on a piece of paper. I wrote, "Andi, I miss you." Then on the next line, I wrote, "It's hard to describe Andi. Her face gets all fuzzy in my mind. She has dark brown hair that seems to have a life of its own. Her eyes are kind of green, but kind of gray—depending on the outfit she has on. And her voice . . . it's kind of low and soft. Except when she giggles. Which is all the time. Was all the time. You see, it'd hard to describe my best friend Andi. Because she's gone. And she's never coming back."

I wrote and wrote, filling up two, then three, then four sheets of paper. As I wrote, I cried. But when I was finished, I felt strangely peaceful. My eyes scanned over what I'd just written. It was good. It said what I felt. If I'd felt like giving a dedication, this is what I would have said.

* * * * *

The Friday of the freshman dance, Bradley turned to me just after the bell signaling the end of lunch period blared.

"You're not going to the dance tonight, I take it," he said.

It was a statement, not really a question. But I shook my head. "No, I'm not."

"Me neither," Bradley said.

I started fiddling with this silver ring my Grandpa Pete had given me after one of his trips to Mexico last summer.

"Can I come over to your house tonight?" he blurted out. "You can say no if you want."

I didn't say no. I nodded. Somehow, it felt right. I definitely didn't want to be at the freshman dance, delivering a dedication. But I didn't want to be at home, having my parents watch me, waiting for me to be comforted or whatever it was that they thought they were doing. I didn't want to have to fight off suggestions that I talk over my grief with perfect strangers. I didn't want to just sit there dealing with the twins, either.

So that was how on the night of the freshman dance Bradley Price came over, and we watched some stupid old movie about a mutant insect who ate whole countries at a time. We popped popcorn and endured a barrage of questions from Jared and Matthew . . . and waited together for Andi.

Nine

THE Monday after the dance, I arrived at school early. As I dragged toward the library, I realized why I'd gotten up so early, knowing I would have to face an icy dawn. It was so I could get my books from my locker before anyone saw me, and dart into the library and get a table in the back. In the back, I could be invisible. No one would stare at me and wonder why I didn't go to the dance or give the dedication.

I wondered if Melissa had stood before the group and said a few words about Andi. What could she possibly have said? Suddenly it made me mad to think that Melissa would even try. Yet a little voice inside me said, "Well, you didn't do it, so someone had to."

Once at the library, I tried to shut off that voice and find something to do. It wasn't easy. There wasn't anyone to write notes to and no homework to do. I spun the globe idly. Finally, I wandered up and down the book aisles until I found something I could read for extra credit in English. I gave it a try, but it was impossible to concentrate. It seemed more appealing just to look out the window and watch the snow that was starting to fall.

My second grade teacher had told us a zillion years ago that each snowflake was different. I wondered how anyone knew. After all, no one had examined every snowflake that had ever fallen. I looked down and toyed with the crystal snowflake hanging around my neck. My dad had given it to me when I was seven. It seemed so long ago that I was seven. Everything had been much easier then.

After a while other students began to fill the library. At each squeak of the double doors, I scrunched down in my seat, hoping no one would notice me. If even one person came over and asked where I was Saturday night, I didn't think I could stand it.

But no one paid any attention to me. The other kids sat down, peeled off their parkas and whispered together in pairs. It was weird how everyone else had something to do. A purpose. A reason for being here.

I watched some girls a few tables away. They were laughing and whispering, and watching a guy at the next table. The librarian frowned at them a couple of times. Then their gaze turned toward me. They turned back and resumed whispering. I couldn't hear what they were saying, but I knew it had to be about me. They didn't know me, but it didn't matter. A lot of students didn't know Andi either, but they'd been talking about her for weeks. And now they were whispering about why Andi's best friend wouldn't stand up and speak at a dance that was dedicated to her.

Why didn't I? Was it simply because I missed her so much I couldn't deal with going to the dance when she wasn't there? Was it because I was too scared to get up in front of everyone? Was it maybe because I'd been jealous that Andi had planned to attend the dance with Bradley, and now I felt guilty because she didn't go with him after all?

I turned inward, searching desperately for the answer. It took a minute, but then it hit me. Maybe it was because I was afraid. That was it. I was afraid the entire student body of Riverview High School wanted me to make sense of why a fifteen-year-old girl had to die. And I *couldn't* make any sense of it. None at all. It was horrible. It was unfair. Why should a drunk guy get to live when he took someone else's life? What was he thinking, anyway?

I closed my eyes and pictured sitting in the darkness of a car, coming home from a movie with my family. Then the bright lights of an oncoming car. Did the driver even see Andi's car? Or was he so drunk he wasn't even aware of it? Why did Andi's car have to be there the exact minute a drunk driver was going the opposite way?

Suddenly I sat up straighter. My mind flashed back on something. Andi had asked me to come to the movie with her and her family that night! What if I'd gone? I might have taken a little longer pulling on my jacket after the movie was over. Maybe the Morelands would have taken just a little longer loading all of us into the car. Andi's brother hated sitting on the hump. Maybe that night he would have insisted that there was no way he was going to sit in the middle. We'd all have scrambled around so he could have a window. So then we would have been on the road just a little later, and the drunk driver would have been going down Fifth Street earlier, before the Morelands had even pulled onto it. He would have careened down the road in the darkness, but it wouldn't have mattered. He would have never hit the Morelands' car. Andi would be here in the library next to me. I'd be helping her with her math homework, and we'd be the ones whispering.

Goose bumps stood up on my arms. *So that was it. If I'd gone to the movies with Andi, Andi would be alive today. It was all my fault!* The realization hit me like a swift punch to the stomach. I couldn't breathe.

"Hey, Kimmie, you okay?" Bradley, his face flushed from the cold, looked down at me. His eyes bored into mine for a second. Then he plunked his books next to me and sat down. "You look . . . wiped out."

"I'm okay," I lied.

"No, you're not," Bradley said gently.

I couldn't meet his eyes again, so I turned away. But then I could see the other students looking at us. Still whispering. Only now there was something else. What were they saying about Andi's best friend and Andi's almost-boyfriend?

In the end, it was safer to look back at Bradley. My eyes traveled over a lock of dark brown hair falling over his forehead, then moved to his shoulders. They were covered by a thick navy coat. If Andi were here, she'd whisper to me, "Check it out. Doesn't he look great in navy?" And I'd have to say, "Yeah."

Only she wasn't there to see him. And it was my fault.

"Do you th-think," I began, then paused. It was too awful to say it aloud. But I had to know, so I tried again. "Bradley, do you think that maybe if I'd gone with Andi to the movie that night, I might have made things run a little . . . say . . . later, and the whole crash never would have happened?"

Bradley's face registered a blank. Then disbelief. "No," he said softly. "You couldn't have changed what happened that night. The only one who could have kept it from happening was that guy who was drunk. You're blaming yourself, and you shouldn't."

I wanted to believe him. But it was hard.

"My dad and I were talking about it last night," Bradley said. "And he said that when something terrible happens, people try to blame someone. It's a way of trying to control something that really can't be controlled. He said most people just can't accept that sometimes . . . stuff just happens."

He leaned over to give me an awkward pat on the shoulder. I slumped in my chair again.

"You know, Andi wanted to be sure I knew that we were going to hang around with you at the dance," Bradley said. "She thought a lot of you."

I nodded slowly. It was nice to hear that. We talked until the bell rang, and our talk blocked the whispers.

Bradley walked me home from school that afternoon. We didn't say much, really. We just stomped through the snow and braced ourselves against a chill wind. But Bradley's presence was comforting.

"I'll come by and get you tomorrow morning and we can walk together," he said as we got to my front walk.

"Thanks," I said shyly. It had been one thing when he just sort of popped up by my locker or had this sudden idea to come over the night of the freshman dance. But now . . . it was too strange. He was making plans. I nodded, said goodbye, and stepped into the warmth of my house. I shook my head, as if to shake out the confusion.

"Hi, Kimmie. We're in the family room."

It was Mom. She must have come home early. I peeked into the family room. She and the twins were sitting on the floor building castles out of interlocking blocks.

"Did your day go okay?" Mom asked, coming over to give me a hug.

I shrugged. There was no way I could tell her how it felt to hide from everyone at school. And I couldn't tell her about how nice it was to be around Bradley, a guy I once compared to a rumpled grocery sack. There were a zillion questions I wanted to ask her, but for now, I had to keep them safely inside my head.

"As days go, this one was okay," I finally said.

"I'm glad. Why don't you take over while I make a few phone calls," Mom said.

"We're not finished with my castle," Jared whined.

"Kimmie, make castles with us," demanded Matthew.

I almost said no. I wanted to go upstairs, turn on my stereo, and think about Bradley and other things. But Jared chimed in too. I set my book bag and parka on the sofa and sat on the floor with my brothers. The walls of the castles rose higher and higher in blues and reds and greens.

Actually, playing with Jared and Matthew wasn't so bad, I decided after a while. It was refreshing to concentrate on something that had a definite beginning and end. Something that didn't leave a person guessing and wondering.

But that night, I did ask my mom whether she thought that maybe I could somehow have prevented the accident.

She shook her head and smoothed my hair and sighed. "Kimmie. Are you sure you don't want to go to that grief support group? Aunt Catherine insists that it really helped her understand the whole process of grief after Uncle Randy died. She talked about how people often have terrible guilt feelings after the death of someone close."

I shrugged. "Maybe. Maybe one day I will." I felt better. Just knowing that lots of people felt guilty after someone died kind of helped. Somehow.

* * * * *

As promised, Bradley stopped by in the morning to walk me to school. And after school, he showed up at my locker and offered to walk me home too. The sun was shining, and it glinted off the snow as we walked.

Somehow we started talking about dogs.

I told him about the funny things Basil had done when he was a puppy, and he told me about his Airedale terrier, Dylan.

"You know, Andi had a lot of animals," I said slowly, almost reluctant to bring up her name.

"Yeah, I heard about some of them," Bradley said, nodding. "Sounds like she had a farm."

"I wonder how they're doing," I added. This was the first time I had thought about the parade of pets that came and went in Andi's life—like Mwoop, who needed a friend. I even found myself wondering what became of that stupid white rat.

"You haven't been over there at all?" Bradley asked. He seemed surprised.

I shook my head. "Let's go by Pet City," I said suddenly. "I . . . I want to see if they have a new shipment of guinea pigs."

"Sure," he said, smoothly switching directions with me.

We had no more than stepped through the doorway of Pet City when Vincent the parrot screeched, "Take a chill pill!"

Bradley laughed.

The commotion brought Mrs. L over. She gave me a sad smile. "How have you been, Kimmie?" she asked.

Her silvery gray hair was sort of tangled, and her glasses dangled unevenly from a chain around her neck. I was glad to see she hadn't changed.

"I'm okay," I mumbled. "I brought Bradley here to see the guinea pigs."

Mrs. L nodded. "There are only three left from the original litter, and they're really huge by now."

"This black-and-white one's cute," Bradley said, holding up a half-grown guinea pig and stroking its soft fur.

Nodding, I reached over and scratched the creature behind its ears.

"Let's go check out the parrot," Bradley said. He set down the guinea pig and wandered toward Vincent.

"Careful. He bites," I warned him.

Bradley smiled at the bird, then slowly held a finger out. In a split second, Vincent snapped at him, and Bradley jumped back.

"No, no, not like that," I said, rushing over. I made soft kissy noises to Vincent and reached out slowly, coming under Vincent's beak. I'd seen Andi do this a thousand times, and Vincent had loved it. When I'd tried it before, Vincent had bitten me. This time, he didn't. He stretched his neck forward and preened.

"He likes you," Bradley said.

I walked down the aisle and stopped to look at some chew toys for dogs. Maybe I'd buy one for Basil. There'd been a lot of rain this winter, and Basil always looked so forlorn when he couldn't race around.

"Think fast," said a voice behind me.

I spun around just as Bradley lobbed me a rawhide football. I tried to catch it, but missed.

"Fumble!" yelled Bradley loudly.

My cheeks heated up when I saw Mrs. L staring.

I picked up the football and shot a warning look at Bradley. He flashed me a grin. Suddenly I felt very uncomfortable. I mean, here I was in Andi's second home, the pet store. Mrs. L had shown me the guinea pigs that Andi had wanted to buy. And I was goofing around with Andi's almost-boyfriend. I felt like an impostor, like I was masquerading as Andi. What kind of a best friend was I? A new kind of guilt poured through me.

I stood up abruptly. "I've gotta go," I said, and I bolted out of the pet store.

Ten

I stayed home from school for the next two days.

"It's my stomach," I told my parents. I thought they were convinced, especially because I hardly ate anything and I stayed in bed the whole time, reading mysteries.

"It's your heart," my mom countered gently the morning of the third day. She pulled the covers off me and stood there with her hands on her hips. "Punkin, you're going to have to face life and keep going." She walked over to my closet and picked out something for me to wear, like I was six years old.

I walked slowly to Riverview that day, and for many days. The walk was lonely, but I didn't dare admit that I missed Bradley. And the thing is, in a weird way I was getting *used* to loneliness. I was getting used to having my locker all to myself. To sitting by myself in the cafeteria or the library at lunch. And to coming home in the afternoon and having no one to talk to.

But getting used to the loneliness . . . that's not all that seemed weird. Here I was in this huge school where you'd think it would be easy to avoid certain people. But everywhere I turned, I'd bump into Bradley. So I'd turn and walk in the opposite direction even if it made me take longer to get where I was going. Once, I caught the hurt in his eyes. For some reason, it just plain made me mad. I hadn't meant for Andi's boyfriend to start liking me. I hadn't planned on liking him, either. I had enough confusion to handle.

At lunch a week after I'd bolted from him, I bought a sandwich at the snack shack and turned toward the farthest corner of the cafeteria. Just as I was making my way there with my tray, someone tapped me on the shoulder. I almost didn't stop, expecting to find Bradley's puppy dog eyes pleading with me. But, no, it was Amy.

Oh, great, I thought. Was she going to corner me and ask me about the dance? I had hoped by now that everyone would have forgotten it.

"Hey, Kimmie," she said, "do you want to come sit with us?"

This was a new one. I glanced at the table where Melissa and the other cheer-leaders were huddled. Then I glanced at the table nearby where Andi and I used to sit. It had long ago been taken over by some nerdy boys. It was like Andi and I had never been there at all.

Turning back to Amy, I asked flatly, "Why?" I balanced my tray on the corner of a table for a second and adjusted my book bag. It weighed a ton. I rarely stopped at my locker because I didn't want to bump into Bradley. Now I carried practically every textbook I used.

"There doesn't always have to be a why, does there?" Amy asked. She tilted her head and gave me this long look. Her face looked open and inviting, and I was struck by a friendliness that I hadn't been aware of before. She had always just been part of mean Melissa Hendricks in my mind.

I shrugged. "I guess not."

"Come on."

Amy led the way. A couple of the girls looked curiously at me, but then went back to their conversations. Every so often Amy tried to include me by asking a question. And one or two of the other girls smiled. They were encouraging me to talk, and I was trying, but my words sounded forced.

I knew everyone was trying to be nice, but if Andi were here, I wouldn't have to work so hard. I could just sort of sit there. She would handle the conversation, and I could just slip in a few comments here and there.

Before long, I felt a headache start. The girls' laughter roared in my ears. And then I caught a look in Melissa's eyes. Probably she was still waiting—waiting for me to explain why I didn't show up for the dance.

It was time to say it straight out: "You want to know the real reason why I didn't do the dedication for the dance for Andi." There.

Amy glanced at Melissa, then nervously twirled her long blond hair. "No," she said swiftly. "People understand."

Melissa looked at the floor. Suddenly the bell rang. I jumped up quickly. Melissa and her friends gathered up their books and said goodbye, joining the throngs of students working their way out the door.

Amy hung back and waited while I

dumped my tray. "About the dedication . . . I think I understand," she said. "And anyway, I think that if you wanted people to know, you'd have told them. Your feelings are your own, and it's not like you're obligated to tell everyone everything. You'll talk about it when and if you want to."

I smiled. "It's nice to hear you say that."

We started down the hall. "Well, it's true. And anyway, it was kind of nice to talk to you." She got quiet for a minute. Then she said shyly, "I hope you don't mind me saying it, but I always wanted to get to know you better. It's just that you were always so busy." She hesitated, then said, "With Andi."

"What do you mean?" I was puzzled. Of course. What else would I have been doing?

"Well, you used to be involved in things around school, like when we were all in elementary school. But then later, you just sort of did things because Andi was doing them. I used to wonder if you ever felt, well . . . submerged."

I paused. I'd kind of started to figure this out before, the night Aunt Catherine took me to dinner. I guess I *had* stopped doing a lot of things, mostly so I could hang around Andi more. Andi hadn't liked things like drama class or the school newspaper. She would just ask me why I wanted to work so hard. It made it easier to forget about them.

"Thanks for asking me to eat lunch with you," I said to Amy as we parted ways in the crowded hall.

"Join us again tomorrow," Amy said. Then she stopped. "And, you know, a bunch of us are getting together at Planet Pizza after school tomorrow. Why don't you come? I'll meet you at your locker."

I shook my head. "Thanks, but I . . . I couldn't. I have to watch my little brothers."

Amy waved her hand. "No explanations necessary. Some other time."

She was gone. I turned around and headed to my next class.

I had two more near misses with Bradley that afternoon, but managed to avoid eye contact.

As I walked home that afternoon, I found myself silently chanting, "Why, Andi, why?" with each footstep. The farther I walked, the sadder I got. It had been fun talking and laughing with other girls. Maybe, I thought, I *hadn't* gotten used to being lonely after all. Maybe—just maybe—I *should* take Amy up on her offer to get together. Just . . . once.

That night, I called Amy to say I wanted to join her for pizza the next day after all. When I hung up, I silently apologized to Andi. I felt like I'd betrayed her somehow.

* * * * *

My classes crawled the next day. When they were finally over, I couldn't believe how quickly I made tracks to my locker to meet up with Amy. In a minute, I was part of a group of laughing, giggling girls. They chattered nonstop as we walked to Planet Pizza.

So did I. I talked with Melissa, then Shannon and Charley and a couple of guys from my science class. It was actually kind of . . . fun. I found myself telling them about the summer I flew to Florida to visit my Grandma Jean, who'd divorced Grandpa Pete a while back. Somehow, I managed to walk on as an extra in a movie that was being filmed near her house.

Melissa looked at me enviously and demanded that I tell her all the details. It was weird. Me—Kimberly Bowen—in the spotlight. But . . . I kind of liked it.

"We're glad you could come," one of the

girls said to me when it was time to go home.

I thought about a lot of things when I finally got up to my room. I wondered what Andi would say if she saw me hanging out with the cheerleaders, talking and laughing. I'd always been so shy. And when it got down to it, lately I was so busy thinking about missing Andi that I hadn't ever stopped to think that maybe all the time I was with Andi, I'd missed out on some things because I'd always been . . . well, in Andi's shadow.

It wasn't her fault, of course. It was mine. And if Andi were there, she'd explain it in a way that made sense. But she wasn't, so there I was, left with even more unanswered questions.

Eleven

THE next morning, raindrops were splashing against my window. Ugh. More bad weather. I took a while dressing, carefully choosing a burgundy sweater and my best jeans.

When I went downstairs, everyone was sitting around the kitchen table eating hot oatmeal. After Mom left with Jared and Matthew, I sat by the front window on the couch. The rain had stopped, and the sun was coming out. I watched and waited. Then, about the time I figured that Shannon and Charley would be walking down the street, I jumped up, grabbed my book bag, and headed for the corner. Sure enough, there they were.

Shannon waved when she saw me. I waited under a wet tree while they walked toward me, not even minding when a few drops splashed down on my parka.

"Hi," the girls called as they got closer. Their eyes were sparkling and when they talked, their breath made little wispy puffs. I fell into step beside them.

"What's up?" I asked, as if it were the most natural thing in the world to walk to school with them.

"I was just telling Charley that I got a call last night from Jennifer Richardson," Shannon said excitedly. "She found out that the drama class is going to announce auditions for a new spring play. It's going to be a musical."

Drama again. A musical. It sounded, well . . . interesting. Scary, yes. To be in front of people, having them watch you. But interesting. Like going on the high roller coaster, knowing you were going to be scared, but thrilled at the fear anyway.

"Do you . . . do you think I could try out even though I haven't been involved in drama before?" I blurted. The second I said that, I couldn't believe it. Shy Kimmie Bowen wanting to get out there in front of people?

Shannon nodded enthusiastically. "Sure, why not? The drama club advisor's always asking us to recruit more members."

Charley and Shannon fell back to talking about other things, but I continued to think about the musical. I felt a new bounce in my step as we got to Riverview High and went our separate ways. But the bounce turned to a dull thud when I arrived at my locker and saw Bradley there. He was waiting. Not for Andi, but for me.

This time, there was no avoiding him. It was still early, so there weren't many people around. The hallway echoed with the sound of my footsteps as I drew closer. I took a deep breath and stopped in front of him, realizing all over again just how tall he was. My eyes were drawn to a red design on his ski parka. It kept me from having to look at his face, where I knew I would see the hurt that I had put there.

"Why have you been avoiding me?" he asked. "It's more than a week now."

I stood rooted to the floor, listening to his words echo in the hallway. What could I say? I've been avoiding you because I like you? And you like me?

"Kimmie, I know the whole thing's weird," he said in a low voice. "I was just getting to know Andi, and then . . . and then she was gone. And at first, I was trying to find her again through you. But then I realized she wasn't there anymore. And I realized something else."

I put my finger up to his lips to shush him. I didn't want to hear more. "Don't say a word," I said. "It's not fair. Not fair to Andi."

"Don't you think I thought about whether it was fair to Andi?" he said, rushing on.

Out of the corner of my eye, I saw Melissa appear at the end of the hallway. She was in her blue-and-white cheerleading outfit, her sweater exactly like the one still hanging on the back of my chair. Her head jerked up, and she seemed to sniff the air like a curious rabbit. Kimmie Bowen and Andi's almost-boyfriend? I could imagine what she must be thinking.

I wanted someone to beam me off the planet right then and there. I wasn't used to soap opera dramatics. That had always been Andi's thing. What would she do? Suddenly I knew. She *wouldn't* shrink up, waiting for Melissa to barrel in and mix things up even further. She'd take things in hand and handle them on her own terms.

"Come on, Bradley," I said firmly, taking his arm and maneuvering him through the hall. My face burned from the force of Melissa's eyes searing through me.

Bradley and I walked silently until we went around a corner. Then I turned around to face him.

"I'm sorry," I said right off. I focused on the red design on his jacket again. It was easier that way. "I wasn't avoiding you because I wanted to hurt your feelings. It's just that, well, I didn't know what to do. Things were getting totally strange. Nothing was supposed to be this way. It wasn't supposed to be you and me."

Bradley shrugged helplessly. "No, but it's the way it turned out. No one asked our permission. And we didn't give anyone permission to take Andi from us, but here we are."

Tears started blurring my eyes, and I looked up, hoping somehow that would stop them from splashing down my face and totally humiliating me. But it didn't.

Bradley reached over and wiped them away, then kind of gathered me up in a hug. I got ready to push him back, but found myself collapsing into the hug instead. I stayed there for a while, sobbing against the warmth of his jacket, not caring who might be walking past and making mental notes.

Finally, I pulled away and dabbed my

eyes, like it mattered by then. I had applied some mascara that morning and it was probably running down my face. Oh, who cared? Nothing made sense anymore, anyway.

"So is it okay? Can you and I be friends, and maybe, someday, more than friends?"

"I don't know yet, Bradley," I said, touching my cheek where the warmth of his jacket had been. It was all too much. "I just don't know." But I pressed my hand on his cheek. "Look, I have to go."

I walked away and headed for the safety of my first class.

Bradley didn't make a point of trying to find me later. I tried to put him out of my mind, and I marched briskly to the drama class just before lunch. I talked to the faculty advisor, Mrs. Ryals. She said I could join. It was that simple.

At lunch, I ate with Shannon and Charley and stopped at Amy's table to say hi. Melissa watched me intently, looking for a clue as to what had happened between me and Bradley. But I didn't let on. Why should I? Anyway, I didn't know the answers myself.

Confused again! I muttered to myself as I started home that afternoon. I was always confused these days. Ever since Andi had left, I never knew what to do about anything! As I walked, my footsteps seemed to say, "Why, Andi, why?"

When I got to the corner of my street, I didn't turn down it. Instead, I went to Andi's street. There, where it always stood, was her house. It was still there. And her bedroom window was still there. And I got mad. All the sadness and confusion of the past few weeks got tangled into a huge knot.

"Okay, Andi," I shouted at her house. "This time, I'm really mad at you! You never come over or answer your phone. Do you think I liked talking to your stupid answering machine all the time?"

There was no answer. "You left your stupid cheerleading sweater at my house. What am I supposed to do with it? Or your boyfriend who I never was supposed to like?" My voice rose higher and higher. "Why did you have to go and leave me? I'm your best friend, you jerk. What kind of a thing is that to do to a friend?"

I picked up this newspaper that was at the end of her driveway and heaved it at the window, nearly breaking it. Andi's mom came to the window and saw me.

"I don't care if you get me into trouble!" I shouted.

When I got home, Mom didn't say anything to me. But I knew she knew what I had done. She hugged me, and she held me while I sobbed.

"Honey, I know it's hard. But you've *got* to go on living," she whispered over and over. "Andi would have wanted that."

"I hate her. I hate her! I hate her!" I shouted, my body trembling.

Nowhere in Aunt Catherine's books and articles did it say what you were supposed to do when you hated someone who had just—zot—disappeared like that. So I had no choice but to go on hating her.

* * * * *

It got to be like a habit with me. For the next couple of weeks, I went on hating Andi. The more I hung around with Shannon and Charley, the more I hated her. I hated her as I auditioned for a part in the school musical. I hated her when I avoided Bradley. I hated Andi when I got a singing part in the musical, and I called Andi's phone number without thinking, only to remember that her answering machine had long ago been disconnected. I hated Andi whenever I thought about her—which was all the time.

I hated her even more the sunny April afternoon that Mrs. Moreland came over and brought me a big box of things that were Andi's.

"She would have wanted you to have these," Mrs. Moreland said to me. Her eyes were watery, and I had to look away before my own eyes overflowed. "It's got some pictures, and the floppy dog that you gave her for her birthday, and some books. You know—things."

Mom was nice enough to take the box and tell me that she'd give it back to me when I was ready.

Mrs. Moreland then handed me another smaller box with holes punched in it. "I don't know if you want to take this on," she said, looking over at my mom. "Alex has taken over Andi's pets, but Mwoop hasn't thrived. Alex suggested—" her voice faltered. "Alex suggested that you try and see if you can bring some spark back to Mwoop."

Me? What did I know about guinea pigs? Lifting the lid on the box, I peered in. Little brown eyes stared back at me. Gently, I touched Mwoop's soft coat, and was startled to feel his tiny ribs.

"He just won't eat much," Mrs. Moreland said.

"Pig pellets," I said firmly, then stopped.

I finally agreed to take him. Mrs. Moreland talked to me about his care. Then my mom led her into the kitchen. I sat on the floor and petted Mwoop, all the while sadly aware that Mrs. Moreland didn't laugh the entire time she talked with my mom.

"We all miss her," I said softly to Mwoop. Poor lonely little guy.

"Oh, Kimmie," said Mrs. Moreland as she was leaving, "there's one more thing. The morning . . . after we all got back from the hospital, this note you'd left was waiting. Alex read it."

I flinched. The letter was all about Bradley and how I felt he was messing with our friendship. How embarrassing that Alex had read it!

"It . . . that was a long time ago," I muttered.

Mrs. Moreland handed me another note. "Andi had written this one to you on Friday, just before we left for the . . . the movie. I found it on her desk. I didn't read it."

I took the note. At first I wasn't going to read it in front of my mom and Andi's mom. But they were looking at me. I decided it would be okay.

The note, in Andi's handwriting that I knew almost as well as my own, said only a few words: "K—I'm sorry if you're sad. I'd never hurt your feelings. Friends Forever—A."

Just like that. So Andi hadn't left me in the middle of a fight. It had been over with before that awful man had hit the Morelands' car and made it so that I couldn't be with Andi ever again. A huge weight lifted off my chest.

"It's okay," I said over and over, my eyes filling. "Things are okay between us again."

Mrs. Moreland nodded. She understood. Later, I watched through the window as she pulled away in her car. For the first time it struck me that I'd lost a best friend, but that the Morelands had lost a vital part of their family. Mrs. Moreland had lost her only daughter. I decided I would visit the Morelands from time to time. Maybe I could make Mrs. Moreland feel better, the way she had for me those mornings before school when my mom had already left for work.

Maybe I could . . .

All of a sudden, I was just plain tired of thinking about things. I needed a break. I needed not to think at all.

I wandered into the family room and decided to watch TV. Maybe it would fuzz out my mind. I found the remote control for the TV wedged between two cushions on the couch and flicked it on. The twins must have been watching some video cartoon because the TV was still set for video. But when the image blurred onto the screen, I saw that it wasn't a cartoon at all. It was the video of my mom and dad dancing to "their" song.

I watched for a few seconds, but just when I was about to turn it off, the scene suddenly changed and there was Andi. I caught my breath. It was the dance video we'd made all those afternoons ago. Andi and I were dancing to "Let's Go Wild!" We were tossing our heads and moving like crazy.

I fumbled with the remote control and put the video on pause. Then I studied Andi, now frozen on the screen. She was laughing, and her eyes were sparkling. I walked up to the screen and tried to touch her face. The electricity went from the screen to my fingertips, causing the little hairs on my arm to stand up. With a snap, I turned off the video and bolted to my room, where I lay on my bed and stared out the window.

I thought about a lot of things, not trying to block them anymore. I thought about how there on the screen, Andi seemed so alive. About someone who'd had too much to drink and had decided to drive anyway. About the dance and how I couldn't give a dedication for my best friend.

Then my mind flashed to the paper I had written about Andi. It was still there in my notebook, in front of my homework assignment sheet. So maybe I wasn't ready to get up in front of people and talk about Andi. But maybe I could give the paper to the editor of our school newspaper and see if it could be published. I could talk about Andi on paper. That would be my dedication to her.

Twelve

TREES everywhere were beginning to form little green buds. Spring was definitely here. Geez. It was weird that an entire season could just kind of creep up on you, almost unnoticed. Time just went right on by, even if the people who should be sharing it couldn't anymore.

Maybe I was thinking about time passing because I found myself a lot busier. The editor at the school paper said he would use my paper on Andi before the end of the month, but first I felt like I had to make it as perfect as I could. I didn't want anyone but me messing with the words.

And then there was Mwoop. I swear he almost kept me on the go as much as Andi did. His spirit was returning, but that wasn't enough for me. I was determined to bring the shine back to his coat.

Maybe that's why the sign in the Pet City window practically shouted when I spotted it after school a few days later: "Spring Pet Sale!" I pressed my nose against the glass to see inside better. There were a bunch of guinea pigs frolicking in the shavings. One of them looked just like Mwoop. Suddenly, I knew what I had to do.

A few minutes later, I walked out, carrying a box with holes punched in it and some new guinea pig pellets. I stepped up my pace. I had to hurry and introduce Mwoop to his new friend. He'd waited an awfully long time for one.

The two guinea pigs took to each other right away. I called the new one Desert Dog, after Andi's duck. I wasn't very good at names, so I had to borrow one of hers.

It didn't take long for Mwoop to get back his whole appetite and fill out. His brown coat started to take on a gloss.

"You were right, Andi," I whispered one day. "Mwoop needed a friend."

And so do I, I thought, glancing sadly at Andi's cheerleading sweater. I looked longingly at my phone, wishing I could call and talk to her. I'd even settle for listening to her answering machine.

Just then, Matthew and Jared burst into

my room without knocking. What else was new?

"We want to play with the guinea pigs," Matthew demanded.

My mouth opened to yell, "Get out and leave me alone." Instead, I was surprised to hear myself say, "Okay. Go ahead. But be very gentle." I sat on the floor with them and told them stuff about guinea pigs.

The next morning, I woke up and showered and got ready for school as usual. And walked outside. And walked past Andi's house, where flowers seemed to be blooming everywhere. And tripped over a crack in the sidewalk.

My notebook went flying. I stood up and realized I'd run my pantyhose and skinned my knee.

Grumbling to myself, I bent over to pick up the papers that had flown all over the sidewalk. I stopped when I saw a piece of rainbow stationery with Andi's familiar handwriting and doodles on it. I started to read her words—words about friendship and being there forever for each other, no matter what. It wasn't the words that startled me. It was that as I read, I could hear her voice in my head, reading the words to me. It was like she was right there with me.

I couldn't read very far, because before long, I started to cry. Only this time, when I stopped, I could think again. And I could picture Andi's face clearly in my mind. And I could remember how she used to laugh, and I realized how much a part of me she still was.

We were friends forever—no matter what.

Somehow, it was okay to admit that Andi wouldn't be coming back ever again. Because I knew that Andi was still here—would always be here. Because, after all, we were best friends.

I stared at her house for a minute. Then I bent over and picked a bunch of orange and yellow flowers that were growing from the crack in the sidewalk. Walking up to Andi's window, I gently laid them on her window sill. A stillness came over me, and I let out a deep sigh.

Then I turned toward school. I wanted to go find Bradley, and to tell him that everything was okay now.

For real.

TO GET HELP

If you're trying to cope with the loss of a loved one, or you know someone who is, there are a number of ways you can get help. Your school principal, a teacher, or a guidance counselor can put you in touch with people who can offer assistance. Church or synagogue groups also can provide support.

Another place you can call is the Grief Recovery Institute's toll-free national help line at 1-800-445-4808, open Monday through Friday from 9:00 A.M. to 5:00 P.M., Pacific Time.

About the Author

Karle Dickerson is the managing editor/operations manager of a young women's fashion and beauty magazine based in California. She lives with her husband, two children, and too many animals—two dogs (a golden retriever and a great Dane), three cats, one Welsh pony, two parakeets, two mice, and a goldfish.

"I first decided to be a writer when I was ten years old and got my first poem published in a local newspaper," Ms. Dickerson says. "I wrote almost every day in a journal from that day on. I still use some of my growing-up situations that I jotted down then for my book ideas and magazine articles."

Ms. Dickerson spends her spare time at Little League games and buying pet food and supplies.